T.R.A.P
To Rise and Praise

Asia Scurry

ASIA SCURRY ENTERPRISES LLC

ISBN: 0692710187
ISBN-13: 978-0692701089

This is a work of fiction. Any references or similarities to actual
events, real people, living or dead or to real locals are intended to
give the novel a sense of reality. Any similarity in other names,
characters, places and incidents is entirely coincidental.

10 9 8 7 6 5 4 3 2 1

Printed in the United States of America

Acknowledgements

First I want to thank God for everything he has done to get me to this step in my life to write this urban fiction novel. On December 13, 2015, I've received the word from God to write this book. It was prophesied that I'll be writing this book and I found it odd because I've never, in all my life imagined myself writing a book. The story behind this book is amazing and I know it will touch many.

Mom, I want to thank you for being my backbone throughout the process of writing my book. You've always been proud of me, encouraging me, and my biggest supporter though it all. I've watched you get more excited about it than I have and you're the reason I've pushed through, other than my kids. I love you.

Semir, I want to thank you because other than my mother, you've been my right hand though everything; from helping me with little ideas and details on the plots to listening to me complain and get aggravated, stopping me from giving up and encouraging me to go forward with this. You've stayed up late nights talking to me about the book and your excitement for me to release it. You and my babies, Semia and Semir Jr, have been my motivation. Thank you so much, I love you babe.

Aunt Veronica, you've been a HUGE help throughout this journey. You helped me research, switch up a few things, as well as, keeping me excited about everything. You've taught me so much. You just don't understand how much I appreciate you and how grateful I am to have you as my aunt.

I also want to thank the rest of my family for being there for me and for supporting me. I'm so happy to be able to make you all proud of me, especially my grandfather Charlie Sr. To see the look on your face when we discuss the book is EVERYTHING I've ever wanted. To my friends, too many to shout out, thank you guys as well.

Enjoy T.R.A.P ''To Rise and Praise''

Prologue

Lauren

How can you out hustle a hustler? You can't beat a boss chick and you can't tell a grown woman anything when she's on her game, well, that's what she thought. Growing up in the streets of Miami, you had to be tough to survive. Everyone and everything around Lauren was moving in the fast lane and she wasn't slowing down for anyone; not her sister or her parents. Even Jesus couldn't catch her if he tried.

She was raised in a family of clean, Christian souls; at least that's what they made you think. Her mother, Eve, was a godly woman and a teacher. Her father, James, was a construction worker and was one of God's soldiers. Lauren and her sister, Janae, grew up in church and could've known the word like nothing else if they would've paid more attention. Her sister knew the word much more than Lauren so I guess you could say she's almost as holy as her parents.

Their neighbors had animosity towards them and they had no friends because most of the girls in the neighborhood thought they were holier than thou, and where they come from, no boys wanted to be with the good girls. Lauren's mother always called them devils in disguise because they would smile in their face, cut them a slice of pie, and then turn around and stab them in the back with the same knife.

Lauren and Janae were considered the prettiest in the neighborhood with their caramel complexion, long black hair, and baby smooth skin. Janae was the conservative one while Lauren couldn't hold back showing a little skin here and there, especially when mama and daddy weren't around. They were beautiful and they were virgins. You know the ones who young men watched in fascination. If things would have gone according to Lauren's plans, she would've lost her virginity a long time ago with a previous crush, but her parents and Jesus had a master lock grip between her legs. Her dad locked those babies up and threw away the key but she knew her time would come one day.

Her family didn't stay in the crème de la crème of neighborhoods but it also wasn't the slums. It was the typical middle class neighborhood which had nice, green grass in the yard, landscaping worth admiring, and trees with lively leaves. If you actually woke up early and listened hard enough, you would hear the birds chirping as they began their day.

Her father tried hard to keep them away from the cruel world because he knew first-hand what it had to offer. He didn't tell them that but he made it perfectly clear that everything out there was ungodly. From the social media sites which Lauren and her sister could never get on, to the diseases going around. Not to mention the disloyalty and dishonesty in the government and the dog eat dog money hustling world that he didn't want them to know about.

Her sister was into the word of God and getting her education more than Lauren ever was. Everything their daddy told them about the outside excited Lauren more than a little bit. She was mesmerized by his stories and couldn't wait until she was grown enough to get out on her own. She wanted to experience a life that was totally opposite of how she grew up.

When Lauren was a little girl, her mother never missed a chance explaining to her that she was strong and that she had a gift. She always came to Lauren and told her about her dreams and the visions she would have. She explained that God favored her and that he was going to use her for greater things. Lauren always heard what she was saying but she never listened. She didn't care much about what she had to say specifically when she talked about God. She felt that the world was big for a reason and that it had so much more to offer her.

Lauren loved Hip Hop and Trap music! She knew all the latest songs and artists because she would listen to it on her iPod at any opportunity. Her parents had no clue that she was listening to and thinking about the lyrics to these songs so that she could find out how to build herself into the biggest, baddest, boss chick around. She had dreams of being that thick thigh, brown eyed beauty who the rappers wrote songs about and who they had in their videos. She wanted to experience the reality of what these R & B men sang about.

While her family's favorite music is Gospel and Christian, Lauren would have no problem walking around humming trap music. She knew the streets weren't good because her daddy told her so, but she also knew it was definitely somewhere she needed to be. Looking at her life, Lauren knew she had it a lot better than some of the others around her. She knew she was favored over others more too, but one day her entire life changed.

On her sixteenth birthday, she woke up sick with the flu which put her on house arrest where she was tucked away from the world. So, because of this, her daddy chose to give her an inch worth of freedom on her seventeenth birthday. Turning seventeen and finally meeting two, new friends at school, Lauren was excited because they actually took the time to see she wasn't as saved as her family portrayed them to be. That was when ish got real.

On the day of Lauren's birthday, she woke up to the smell of fresh, baked biscuits, hot sizzling bacon, soft scrambled eggs, and her favorite, fluffy homemade from scratch pancakes cooking on the stove. She saw mama whipping it up in the kitchen while daddy was entertaining himself with a rerun of the Miami Heat basketball game from the night before. As usual, Janae was nowhere to be found. Lauren figured her head was probably so far into the books that she didn't realize school was starting in the next hour.

Arriving at school, Lauren was greeted with a handmade card and a few balloons from her good old friends, Samantha and Starr. They were your typical around the way girls. They had just enough good and a little bit of hood, depending on the current situation. They were undoubtedly more mature physically than Lauren and even though they were quite book smart, they were extremely street smart. They both had more friends than Lauren could ever imagine and along with the friends also came a lot of enemies.

It just so happens that they all got an invite from the most popular female at their school, Jessica. That girl was so bad even some of the females in their school had to take a double look, questioning their own sexuality. She's never paid Lauren any attention though. This party was sure to be the party of the year. Everybody and their mama would be out there, with a good share of ballers and baddies everywhere.

The next day, all anyone talked about through the school halls was this party. Her home girls insisted she find a way to go to the party but she knew that under her mother and father's roof there was no way in a Devil's hell she would make it out that house past six. They knew that too but they thought she'll at least get a free pass since it was her birthday after all.

During lunch that day, her girls approached her about spending the night with one of them so she could go to the party with them that way. Hearing this plan had her a little scared but there was no way she could pass up having the chance to get out the house for her birthday weekend. After a few minutes of thinking, she was ready to execute the plan.

That evening, Lauren ran home and asked her parent's permission to spend the night with Samantha. She was so scared; she felt the urge to pee just waiting for their answer and to her surprise, they said, "Yes".

She had to clean her room, the kitchen, and she had to make sure she was back at home that Saturday morning at 11 o'clock on the dot. Lauren did what she had to do and was on her way to Samantha's house around five that afternoon.

When she arrived at Samantha's house, Starr was already there and they both had their coochie cutters, crop tops and their 5 inch heels laid out and ready for tonight's festivities. Lauren was so embarrassed because she only brought a v cut long sleeve shirt, jeans and a pair of retro Jordan's that her uncle left on her bed for her birthday. It was the first pair she had ever owned and she was too excited to rock them out with the girls.

After they all showered up, did their hair and makeup, and put on their banging outfits, Lauren would've been dead if looks could kill that night. When Samantha and Starr saw what Lauren put on, the looks they gave her could've killed a dead man twice. They went in on her hard. Their stares, to Lauren, were a bit much until finally, Samantha stopped and ran to her closet to pull out something a lot sexier. She pulled out the smallest mini dress Lauren had ever seen in her life with some of the highest heels on earth.

She didn't want to tell them that she was too scared to wear those heels because all she could think about was the way her butt would look in that dress and sit up in those heels. Lauren quickly changed and returned to the room. She found pleasure and relished in the stares they gave her now. Their eyes opened so wide, you would've thought they had seen a ghost. She knew she was officially the baddest chick in their little group and she was feeling herself hard. She could barely walk in those heels but she didn't care because she was doing the most.

This was all new to Lauren because she only wore things that showed a little bit of her cleavage. She's worn short shorts before but to attend a party half naked and in an outfit more revealing than a stripper, she couldn't imagine and it made her more nervous than ever.

When they rolled up to the party, Lauren's eyes lit up as they saw huge wheeled cars and trucks, hooked up with the latest rims, the tightest paint jobs, and the loudest speakers you'll ever want to hear. There were so many women walking around wearing outfits more revealing than hers and the men were flocking around them like vultures around a dead animal on the side of the road. The music was bumping and it was her type of music...trap music. She knew every song the DJ played and was honestly ready to rock and twerk her hips to the beat.

As they got out of their car and walked around into the middle of the party, all eyes were on them but let Lauren tell it, all eyes were on her. She was finally starting to feel like one of the sexy, video girls her favorite rappers rapped about and that bad boss chick that she was determined to be. As she turned around to scan the room, she locked eyes with this guy standing by the bar. She instantly felt an unusual spark, an attraction so magnetizing she didn't know what was going on. This was something that she had never felt before. She was intrigued as soon as she laid eyes on him.

He was tall, red, and handsome. He was standing 5'9 with long, dark dreadlocks and some of the smoothest skin that Lauren had ever seen on a man. She noticed his laid back thuggish swag with the gold teeth in his mouth. Everything about him screamed money and Lauren was intent on listening.

At that moment, he was surrounded by four other men and before she knew it, Samantha & Starr ran over to talk to them. Lauren was so busy admiring what could potentially be her future if she presented herself the right way, that she didn't realize she had been standing by herself. Once she came back to reality, she took her time walking to where her girls were sitting. She swayed her hips from side to side so smooth that she could feel his eyes moving with every inch of her curves. He was staring at her so hard he could have burned a hole through her body and soul. She also took her time because she was trying to get used to walking in those bad girl heels that her home girls put her in but no one needed to know that except for her.

Lauren kept her cool as she approached her girls and asked them about getting some punch. She pretended she didn't notice him scanning her up and down with every step she took but she did notice and she enjoyed every bit of it. When she finally turned around toward his way, he introduced himself to her by the name Money. With the way he was dressed and how well kept he looked, she should've known he was going to hit her with a name like that.

With the level of confidence emanating from her that night, she gave him her sexiest smile and most seductive pose. She extended her hand and said, "What's up? My name is Lauren. The baddest chick you'll ever meet and the only one you'll never forget."

She was on ten, with her head held high and her confidence level to the roof. She couldn't believe how bad she was herself but she knew she had him hooked.

He smiled at her with a smile that could put any girl into a trance. He gave her credit on her introduction and from that day forward, Lauren knew exactly what she wanted in her life to make it more exciting.

Money

Travis Williams, better known as Money, was Miami's biggest and baddest dope boy in the streets. Money was only 22 but he was running things like a true OG. He was a hot mix of Puerto Rican and Black. He had much pull, many enemies, and he was a real boss. Being the biggest and baddest around came easy to Money and he made sure that he made it extremely hard for people to get close to him.

He got a lot of his work from across the waters with the help of his father, another well-known OG named Jerry. Money and his father had seen it all and have been through it all, from murder to rape to pimping, there was nothing off limits. Jerry gave Money a rough life but he never turned his back on his dad because of the loyalty he taught him. Jerry stacked his money, settled down, married Money's mother and called the street life quits. Money looked up to his father like none other and would have killed anyone if they had betrayed them.

Money had his share of females. He could get them from left to right. It was so easy for him that he could snap his fingers and one would appear, on the spot, ready to do whatever he needed or to give him whatever he wanted. It didn't move him one bit because his focus was straight tunnel vision. His mantra was always money over hoes, at least until he ran into Lauren three years ago at a teen party.

Jerry tried to keep Money focused and ahead in the game because he knew there was so much money out in the streets of Miami. Sleep wasn't an option and with his father so hard on his back, he barely got any. Their family ran the streets of Puerto Rico, with more than a few heavy hitters and relentless killers on their side. Money wasn't new to the game when it came to killing either. He's a little more experienced than he wants to be when it comes to the skeletons and murders swept into his closet. He never told a single soul outside of those who were with him on those business runs.

The hustlers in the streets of Miami weren't crazy; they knew who was behind a lot of the murders but no one ever snitched because they knew the consequences they would have to face from his do boys, even when he was locked up.

The night Money attended the teen party with his friends; he wasn't focused on anything but building his clientele. He knew that with all the young, gullible addicts he had the advantage to draw in a good amount of business and he was ready. That night went kosher for him as he bopped his head to the music and watched all the young chicken heads make a fool of themselves trying to get his attention. None of them caught his eye until he spotted this fine female. She looked kind of young but that still didn't turn him away.

They locked eyes on each other and it was hard for either of them to turn away. While she walked over to her friends, Money wanted her to notice him checking her every twist and curve, but she seemed unbothered by his stares. That intrigued him because most females threw themselves at him but this one…there was definitely something different about this one. He didn't know what it was about her but he knew he liked it. The way she carried herself and the confidence that exuded from her excited him and she was what he needed. She was everything he wanted and more. That night after he introduced himself to her, she told him her name was Lauren and that she was the baddest chick he'll ever meet and the only one he'll never forget, he knew he couldn't let her get away from him.

Chapter 2

After conversing with Money outside of Samantha's house for four hours in his car, Money handed Lauren his second cell phone. Lauren didn't own a cell phone because her parents were so strict but he wanted her to keep it so that he could always get in touch with her. He had noticed that there was something about her that no one else recognized. She had the potential to be his ride or die chick, but then again, something within him kept telling him to just leave her alone. He didn't listen; he had to have her in every possible way.

There was just something about Lauren. He knew she was his type and he knew that he had plenty of females who would run at his every beck and call but he needed to have Lauren by his side and for the long haul. She was just that type of female.

Money wasn't too fond of Lauren's friends, Samantha and Starr because of the way they carried themselves. Starr carried herself more respectfully than Samantha but they still didn't peak his interest. He knew he wouldn't make conversation with them and he was glad his boys called those thots over so he could have a chance to get closer to Lauren. After spending some time with her, he knew her family was into church and he found out about her family background but that didn't stop him from pursuing her.

Money and his family weren't spiritual or religious. They just lived their life day by day and whatever happened, happened. They didn't pray, say their grace before eating, or even acknowledge any type of God about anything. Money had a lot of enemies and it made Lauren skeptical about talking to him, but, somehow, she felt that maybe he would keep her safe if anything was to pop off.

"Hey babe, what's up, are you hungry?" Lauren said as she answered her prissy, pink iPhone that Money had given to her. She was spending the day with Samantha, Starr, and Janae, at the mall. They were in Linda's Nails getting a manicure and pedicure laughing and joking around when he called. Money spoiled her like it wasn't anything. She enjoyed her weekly mall excursions, especially with her best girls. They all knew how to have a good time when the mall was involved.

"Nah I'm good ma, I was just calling to check in on you and to see where you put the rest of my twenty grand." Money replied.

"Oh I put it back in the safe; I only took what you gave me to shop with and a few more dollars to get you a little something-something!" Lauren said as she smiled, thinking of the Rolex she just purchased for her man. She was so excited to get home to him so that she could surprise him since he didn't know what it was that she had gotten him. She bought some hot as fire red bottom heels for her but ended up surprising Janae with them.

The entire time Lauren and Money were on the phone, Janae stared at Lauren from the corner of her eye. She didn't care for Money that much because she knew what he was about. She thought it was cool that he spoiled her sister because she got a few goodies out of the deal but she always felt something was up with him. There was something that just didn't sit well with her. She wouldn't tell Lauren because she knew Lauren would have an issue so she decided to let things play out however the chips fell.

"Okay y'all, I'm about to run. You know its bible study tonight so I'll see y'all later." Janae said.

While Lauren said her I love you to Money and hung up the phone, she wanted to let Janae know, in her own sisterly way, that she had no life.

"You're always running off to somebody's church behind mama. That's exactly why you don't have a life or a man now." she said with a frustrated tone.

"Lauren, what you fail to realize is the only man I need in my life right now is God. He's the only friend I need too, so yes, I attend church faithfully every Sunday and bible study every Tuesday. Just because you're living this new little life and you've turned your back on God because you think you're this big bad boss chick now doesn't mean you don't need God, Lauren. One day you're going to see that you really do need him more than any and everything."

Suddenly, Starr interrupted the escalating argument and the preaching that was bound to happen between Janae and Lauren. She knew it was going to turn into a huge debate in the middle of the mall and she was not feeling that right here, right now.

"You girls need to chill. We didn't come here for all of this, so, Janae, we will see you later boo. We know your daily routines and I don't understand why your sister always has to start a fight with you about it. Sometimes you just have to ignore her and just keep the peace for your nerve's sake."

Lauren became silent and walked into the next store after paying for her Mani-Pedi. Starr and Janae gave each other a hug and Janae made her way out of the mall. Samantha didn't hear anything and she had no clue of what had transpired between Lauren and Janae as she was extremely focused on her text conversation. Ms. Linda could've cut off one of her toes and she wouldn't have known with the focus she had on her phone.

Starr sat down and leaned over to see what had Samantha's undivided attention. She grabbed the phone to take a quick look and saw the word "new boo" on her text contact. Samantha immediately grabbed her phone back and caught an attitude with Starr for being nosey, but yet she couldn't help but smile because of the butterflies her new fling gave her.

"Who's the new boo?" Starr asked smiling.

"Well, I'm not revealing any names but just know that he got stacks. He's considered single in my eyes, even though he's not and he is just everything to me right now. We have been texting each other all night when he's out handling his business. We text during the day, sometimes, if his future ex-trick isn't around messing up everything. That's all you need to know for now." Samantha laughed.

She was grinning from ear to ear like a queen in a castle, while Starr was trying to figure out why she feels the need to settle for a guy in a relationship. Samantha had no care in the world for her new boo's girl because money talks and she liked the way it sounded. She knew his girl would be out of the picture soon enough and to add insult to injury, she was a home wrecker and had no sympathy for the female in the relationship.

Lauren, Samantha, and Starr's friendship started when they were in school and they've been tight ever since. They did everything together and never skipped a beat talking to each other. In their eyes, they were some of the baddest females to ever grace the school campus. From learning how to do make-up professionally by practicing on each other's faces to keeping up with the latest styles and trends. They always updated each other about what to wear and what not to wear as well as the hottest and sexy slang pick-up lines to get more men. They learned a lot more about the street life hanging around with the groups they hung with.

Lauren knew a little more than Samantha and Starr because she was in a relationship with a dope boy. Money made her street smart and taught her everything she needed to know about how to fire a gun. He made sure she knew about the streets because he wanted to know she was able to protect herself when she wasn't with him. It was mandatory for her if she was to handle his lifestyle.

After Lauren turned eighteen, Money knew that if she was going to be all in with him, he needed to have her under the same roof so he moved her from her parent's home. Her parents were furious about this idea and his influence on her to make her leave their home. They couldn't help but to hate him with every bone in their body but she was an adult and there was nothing they could do to stop her. Also, being Christians, they weren't supposed to hate anyone, but he made it extremely hard not to. All they could really do was pray and let God handle it.

Lauren built her reputation of being a bad street chick but Money never let her steer that way. She was his ride or die but she also worked. She was one of Miami Cities Bank best employees. Money needed everything to look legit so he would've hurt her if she had lost that job. Lauren always dreamed of the hustle and tried to talk to Money about it all the time, but he never listened. He would cut her off and told her to stay focused on legit woman things. He would tell her to let him handle the streets for now. She dreamed of running an all-female mob with her as the queen pin. They would take over the streets like only she could.

"Hey baby, are you in here?" Lauren asked while she walked through her expensive top floor condo.

Lauren's house was laid with the finest. The condo had vaulted ceilings, marble floors, and black and white appliances. She even had an all-white room that no one was allowed to go into. This room was just for the appearance and decor. She was in love with her 3 bedroom, 2 bath condo and even though she didn't acknowledge God, she felt extremely blessed.

Lauren turned around and (SMACK), coming out of nowhere, Money hit her so hard in the face that she dropped her bags and stumbled, almost falling on the floor.

"Who told you to take extra of my money to buy me anything? I don't need you to buy me nothing! You spend what I tell you to spend to keep up with your looks, nothing more, and nothing less!"

Money yelled as he was pacing back and forth in anger.

"Baby I just wanted to surprise you because I haven't surprised you in a while." Lauren replied, holding her face.

Money wasn't hearing anything she had to say. He used to treat her like a queen at the beginning of their relationship. However, after she met his parents, things went downhill. Money loved Lauren but about a year ago, he started putting his hands on her from time to time. Lauren was confused about this sudden change because from the time he met her, he always put her on a pedestal. He still does but then again, he treats her like dog crap sometimes too. She always wondered what made him change all of a sudden.

She was trying to be the woman he wanted her to be. She catered to his every need and never complained. Money was Lauren's first real boyfriend and she lost her virginity to him. She felt that maybe one day he would propose to her because she's stuck with him through any and everything.

Lauren immediately rushed to the bathroom to fix herself back up as Money grabbed his keys and left the house. After she heard his tires screech off, she picked up her phone to call Janae.

"Janae, Money had an episode again and he hit me. It wasn't hard so don't get mad." Lauren said sobbing.

"What do you mean it wasn't hard? You always talk to me about his little flaws and then you try to paint a prettier picture than what it actually is. I'm not stupid." Janae huffed with frustration.

Janae was never fond of Money and she was hoping things would play out without him laying his hands on her sister but she was started to realize the uneasy feeling she had about him wasn't all in her mind. She only knew of Money hitting her sister one other time but one time was too many in Janae's book. Lauren always told her about their arguments but she would try to not make them look as bad as they were.

"Lauren, the first time he hit you, you should've left him but you're grown and dumb and want to follow what's in. That's not how you should live your life, that's not how mom and dad raised you. Listen, I know you aren't going to leave him but let me say a prayer for you." Janae said mustering up the strength to forgive Money.

Lauren's family was always quick to pray about something. She never stopped them because it was rude, but she never really listened either because that wasn't what her mind was set on right then.

"Okay Lauren, I want to read to you Psalms 27:1. The lord is my light and salvation so why should I be afraid? The lord is my fortress protecting me from danger, so why should I tremble? When evil people come to devour me, when my enemies and foes attack me, they will stumble and fall. Though a mighty army surrounds me, my heart will not be afraid. Even if I'm attacked, I will remain confident. Amen".

Lauren said, "Amen" and was instantly trying to get off the phone. She was tired from her day. Janae mentioned to Lauren that God favors her and that she sees it and they said their goodbyes.

Lauren thought about everything her sister said about her polishing up the truth to make it seem better, but she knew she didn't want to tell her family the full details to make them hate Money even more. She was in love with Money and she couldn't see herself with any other man. Money knew that so he took advantage. Lauren showered, got settled into her king sized bed under her purple silk covers, and fell off into a deep sleep. She had dreams every night but she never paid them any attention until tonight. This dream was so clear; it scared her out of her sleep because it seemed so real.

Back at the Jacobs house

On a windy and chilly Sunday morning, Eve Jacobs had the stove going cooking grits, eggs, pancakes, and her famous butter biscuits were rising in the oven. She was worshiping so hard to her Christian worship music playing on her phone, that she didn't even notice her husband James entering the kitchen to come give her a kiss and to eat breakfast.

"Good morning love, how did you sleep?" Eve asked.

James replied saying "I slept great, I missed you this morning but I see you got up extra early to cook huh?" James asked with a smile.

"Yeah you know how I do, can't let my man wake up starving." Eve said.

Eve and James are happily married. They met 21 years ago and had Lauren when they were just boyfriend and girlfriend then they split up. They reconnected later in life and worked things out to get married. They were both into the church deeply because of their hard past and they're devoted to making their children turn to God for any and everything.

"Good morning Mom and Dad." Janae said as she sat at the table looking half asleep.

"Good morning love how was your day yesterday with your sister?" Eve asked.

"Oh it was good, same old Lauren flexing and flaunting her new life with that street punk of hers."

Eve told Janae to watch her mouth, don't bad talk him and just pray for them.

"They will get what they have coming to them, Janae. Money and Lauren know they can't live this lifestyle forever and that's surely not how I raised my child. I should have known she was going to drift off horribly because she never seemed to want to get into the word at church." Eve said wondering what could've happened to her baby girl.

"God has favored her and I've been telling her that since she could comprehend. She's just hardheaded and the devil's riding her but she will learn the hard way."

Janae replied saying "Mama, you know she called me last night and told me Money had another one of his little episodes."

James didn't waste any time turning to Janae to get in tune with the story she was about to tell.

"Yeah ma, when we came from the mall, he hit her but you know she always trying to take up for him and make it seem like he didn't mean to or some stupid crap. I read a scripture to her and prayed for her so hard last night, Mama, because I know the devil is going to attack them. I just can't stand to see my sister this way".

"I know baby." Eve said.

James became furious. Money already took his daughter from their home and taught her the very things James was working hard to keep her from. He almost got her to stop speaking with her own family because of his devilish ways and the control he has over her. James was trying to keep his sanity and leave everything in God's hands but when it came to his first born child, he was ready to bang out with anybody.

James came from a rough thug life too. Before James married Eve and during their first year of marriage, he would hit the streets hard. James was a real thug with tattoos everywhere, females on every corner and slinging crack harder than the jits that call themselves dope boys nowadays. Money had that real work that James was familiar with and James knew Money wasn't a petty gangster. He always wondered how that boy managed to have the streets on lock the way he did and how he got the weight that he moved. He knew Lauren would never tell him though.

James has plenty of skeletons in his closet and turned his heart to the Lord after having a near death experience. With the motivation of his wife and watching her take her first steps into the kingdom of God, it caused him to start going to church.

"I think I'm going to give her a call today and say a prayer or something, I need to hear from her but I know she won't open up with me the way she does for you, Janae" Eve said.

"Okay Ma, she opens up with me but she still sugar coats everything, it doesn't matter what it is. I know she's unhappy but that money he has is keeping her there. On the days when he's nice, she has hope for their relationship and the reputation she built for herself will keep her with him because of who he is in the streets. Hand me my phone." Eve said.

Two minutes later, Lauren answered the phone for her mother.

"Hello." Lauren said with the intention to rush off the phone. "Lauren listen, we have to talk honey. Your sister told me about the little episode Money had last night and the Holy Spirit is telling me that you're in trouble. Lauren, please listen to me and re-evaluate your life."

"Mom, I am okay. Man, y'all always blowing stuff up and Janae always running her mouth. We just got into a little spat and he accidentally hit me. That's all. He apologized about it this morning."

Lauren said knowing she was lying out her teeth because she hasn't seen Money all night or morning.

Eve sensed something different from what Lauren was saying but she didn't want to argue with her. She just wanted to pray. The Holy Spirit was telling her it was so much more than that incident but she didn't know what.

"Okay Lauren, let me just say a prayer and read a verse for you love and I'll let you go."

"Alright Ma go ahead" Lauren said.

"Okay, is your bible close to you because you know I like it when you read along. You feel it more in your soul than just hearing it from me."

"Yes Ma I got it." Lauren lied once again.

"Okay, turn to Romans 12:1-2."

Eve began to read, "and so dear brothers and sisters, I plead with you to give your bodies to God because of all he has done for you. Let them be a living and holy sacrifice, the kind he will find acceptable. This is truly the way to worship him. Don't copy the behavior and customs of this world, but let God transform you into a new person by changing the way you think, then you will learn to know God's will for you, which is good and pleasing and perfect".

"Okay Mom, are we finished because I have to start laundry and I know that you'll be making your way to church soon?" Lauren interrupted.

Eve replied "Yes, we're finished. Just be safe and know that God has you no matter what but he wants you to want him too. You have to want him in your life Lauren. He is your father and he has to be your everything. Look at your life."

"Mom, my life is great. I live in the best condos in Miami, I drive a 2014 BMW, I have a man, unlike Janae, and I got money in my pocket, aren't I blessed?" Lauren replied laughing.

"No, you actually just named all materialistic things that can be taken in a heartbeat. Your man ain't godly and he isn't treating you right. You aren't married, Lauren, so if you want to be technical, and you think you got it on lock when you really don't. Your man ain't your man until that ring gets on your finger while you're trying to flaunt him around and portraying yourself to be this happy female when really you're just pretty and low key miserable. I can't do nothing but give it to you blood raw, shall I continue?"

Eve was about to let Lauren have the whole sha-bang until James saw that the hood was creeping up out of her.

"Alright ma, you can have that one. I'll let you go since you call yourself being "real" now. Holla at you later." Lauren said.

Eve couldn't do anything but roll her eyes but before that phone hung up, she made sure she told her to humble herself.

Chapter 3

It was a bright and beautiful day in the streets of Miami so Starr hit up the girls to see what the day had in store for them. Starr was well off with a great job, a nice apartment and a fresh to death, clean car. She was single and had male friends but she didn't want an exclusive man right now. She was getting over her heartache from a previous relationship and she just didn't want to bother with the whole being exclusive boyfriend and girlfriend issues.

She was a young boss chick with a big booty that all the men flaunted over. She was the different one out the bunch because she considered herself a classy woman with a whole lot of hood in her. She grew up in a well-off home but was a strong headed independent woman who wanted to get everything on her own with no help from her family, and that's just what she did. Not having much family in Miami was hard for Starr because when she needed someone, there was really no one close enough to support her.

All of her family lived in New York except for her grandmother. Her grandmother was in her early fifties and could barely walk because she had a severe and unusual case of arthritis so Starr would go and sit with her on the weekends or when she didn't have to work. She would check up on her to make sure she was doing okay and also so that she could vent when she needed a listening ear. Starr loved her grandmother and would do anything for her especially since she was the only part of her family living here in Miami with her.

Starr called Lauren and as usual, she had to call her later because Lauren was not a morning person, more specifically, she wasn't a morning person on her days off. Since it was Sunday, she automatically put Janae in church with her family. She knew Samantha didn't have anything to do so she headed her way to see what she was up to and what she wanted to do. As Starr reached the second stoplight away from Samantha's neighborhood, she noticed Money's car at the light across from where she was.

She knew it was Money because his car was unique in color and stood out from any other car in the area. He was in the car alone and looked as though he was enjoying his music by the way his head was bopping. The light changed and they crossed paths.

When Starr arrived at Samantha's home, she noticed the door was unlocked so she helped herself inside. The entire living room had the smell of sex and there was weed all over the table. There were three Ciroc bottles on the counter in the kitchen and a couple of glasses. Starr was confused by what she saw but intrigued at the same time because she was curious as to what had happened.

Samantha finally comes to the front of the house, shaking her hair while trying to put it in a ponytail. She had on a silk silver robe and flaunted the biggest smile on her face, singing, extremely loud,

"I'm in loveeeee." Starr laughed but wondered what had happened to the place and where Samantha's little boo thang was.

"Um, Trick, what happened to this place? I see you had a great night." Starr inquired.

Before Samantha could reply, her phone began to ring. She answered grinning from ear to ear.

"What's up baby, did you leave something?"

Starr went to the bathroom and when she came back, Samantha looked confused trying to figure out why her signal was weak and why her phone call disconnected.

"Starr, I'm about to get in the shower and then we can go grab something to eat. I am starving and I have the worse hangover honey."

Samantha strolled to the bathroom leaving Starr on the couch. Starr was about to turn on the TV when she heard Samantha's phone ring with a notification. She knew the sound was from her text messages but paid it no mind. A few moments later, the phone rang and being nosey, Starr leaned over to see who was calling. Her eyes grew when she saw that the caller ID said Money.

Thinking to herself, "Whoa what the, why would Money be calling Samantha's phone?"

Starr didn't trip. She sat back concerned if anything had happened with Lauren and decided to call to make sure things were straight.

Lauren answered and Starr became frantic trying to figure out if she was okay.

"Whoa, Starr, calm down crazy girl! I'm fine. I was doing laundry and my phone was in the room. I put it on vibrate because I've had so many missed calls, it ain't funny."

"Oh okay, just making sure girl. Is Money home?" Starr questioned.

"No, we had a little misunderstanding last night and he hasn't been home since, but come on now, this is his place as well as mine. You know he'll be back."

Starr's curiosity grew as Lauren kept talking but she kept her cool. She didn't mention anything about Money calling Samantha. She was ready to get off the phone with her friend so she could find out what's going on.

"Alright babes, I have a few things that I need to handle, I will hit you up later today okay?" said Starr.

As they both said their goodbyes, Starr heard Samantha turning off the water to get out of the shower. Starr didn't know what to think while she waited for her to come back into the living room. Samantha rushed into her room, wrapped in a big oversized towel singing, "Oooh it's chilly!"

She yelled to the front, "Starr, I'll be up there in a minute! Let me get dressed and all cute and then we can go."

Starr was confused and she started getting angry as all kinds of thoughts played through her head.

"Ain't no way Samantha is screwing with Money knowing that's our girl man!"

She wanted answers and wanted them now. She was feeling some type of way and her face showed it because Samantha felt the vibe she was giving off when she came from the back.

"What's wrong with you, Starr?" Samantha asked while staring at the TV.

"Samantha, why did Money call your phone?"

"Oh, my gosh!" Samantha said as she grabbed her cell.

"He called back? My phone was being so crappy, it disconnected our call."

"So hold up! Wait a freaking minute! When you answered your phone, called your boo baby, and asked did he leave anything, that was Money? I can't believe you! YOU'RE A FREAKING SNAKE IN THE GRASS! How could you do this to Samantha? I know you're a home wrecker but you're doing this to Lauren. She's supposed to be our best friend."

"Girl, calm down! Lauren is YOUR bestie, not mine. We're cool and all, but I mean, she's weak! Why would Money genuinely be attracted to her? He needs someone strong and who could be a real ride or die," said Samantha in her defense.

"Are you serious, Samantha? That's so messed up. You ain't loyal; have you ever done anything like this to me?" asked Starr.

"Heck naw, I am loyal, only to a select few and you're included so don't ever second guess that.

Samantha and Money have been messing around for 6 months. He's been paying her bills, buying her expensive gifts, and even paying her mother's bill in the old folk's home. Money didn't love Samantha at all but she had a great piece of tail that he could get whenever he wanted.

Samantha was always envious of Lauren almost to the point of hating her but she kept her sanity since she was around her so much this past year. Money approached Samantha at a corner store near her house and liked what he saw. She didn't look the same as the night he met Lauren at the party when Starr and Samantha were talking to his boys.

Her breasts got bigger, her butt was nice and plump, and she dressed a tad bit trashy. He saw every curve of her body in her booty shorts and sports bra which is what attracted him to her this particular day. She wasn't as pretty as Lauren but he had no intentions of wifing her. He strictly wanted to hit and he made that known at the store. Samantha knew exactly who he was. She knew whose man he was and what he was made of. She wanted to be his wife and was willing to do anything to get to that point.

Starr knew this whole thing was trouble and didn't want to get in the middle of it, but somehow, she felt she would be. She just didn't want to be there when Samantha and Lauren ripped each other apart. She thought hard about how to tell her friend that her man wasn't worth the ground he walked on. She wanted to know what he was doing with Samantha since Samantha was always in Lauren's face but she had no clue of how to break the news. She grew silent and just kept her mouth closed, at least for now. She knew that what was done in the dark would eventually come to the light.

−Lauren

"OH MY GAWWD!" Lauren screamed. "I'm in love with a man that I know is down for me but ain't worth nothing. If he was really in love with me, he wouldn't lay a finger on me. That's not true love. He keeps me in the dark about certain things but yet shares special moments with me. I've never been more confused about my relationship in my life!"

Lauren sat on the toilet questioning her love life with Money while holding a positive pregnancy test. The entire time she thought about how she was going to tell her family, her friends, or even Money, that she was pregnant. Shocked and worried, she couldn't think of an easy way and definitely didn't want to tell anyone anytime soon. She wasn't even sure if she wanted to keep it but her family would be devastated if she ever had an abortion. They don't believe in abortions and frankly, she didn't either so this will be something she kept to herself for now. She wanted to first make an appointment with her doctor to confirm. Lauren hoped it was all a dream because she had so much on her mind, she could barely think straight about this pregnancy.

As Lauren prepared dinner for herself, thinking how she wanted Money to come back soon, she received a phone call from her job's HR department. She answered the phone only to find out that they called to fire her because of her recent lack of performance and because of the confrontation she had with a coworker. Lauren didn't know what to do at this point. Losing her job, finding out she was pregnant, and telling her man everything was a bit too much for one night. Money was going to kill her and she knew it. They had just gotten into it about some money and then for him to come home and hear all of this would be horrible for her.

Lauren may have been dumb on some things but she wasn't a fool when it came to her bread. She knew she and Money had a lot stashed away but she also wanted to keep her job and money flow going personally just in case something happened to her. She wanted to be financially stable with or without Money. Even though she was in love, she wasn't stupid.

As Lauren was getting ready to take it in for the night, a strong feeling came over her. It was as if she wasn't in the room alone. She had an urge to pray about what's been happening to her since she didn't want to tell anyone else just yet, but she immediately pushed that thought out of her head. She wondered if Money would ever come back and if he still wanted to be with her. The thought of telling him all of this news whenever he walked through the door made her stomach cringe.

She couldn't help but wonder if he would still put his hands on her knowing that she was pregnant. She quickly changed her thinking because if she lost her baby because of him hitting her, she would lose her mind.

While lying in bed, she couldn't help but wonder if he was out in the streets with another female. She knew he didn't like to sleep at his homeboy's house or none of his trap houses so he had to be laid up with some thot. She couldn't help but get over-emotional and all the things going through her mind tonight made her cry herself to sleep.

-Money

"Yoo what's up?" Money said as he answered his phone. "What's up my dude?" Troy said on the other end of the line. "What you got going on tonight, man? I need you to meet me at the spot in about 10 minutes."

"Alright man, 10/4." As Money hung up with his high school friend, his father called. "What's up, Pops?" said Money.

"Nothing much, son, what you up to, young blood?"

"I'm about to hit the spot and check up on Troy, you good old man?"

"Yeah I'm good, how you and your little friend doing? Y'all still on track?"

"Yeah Pops, I'm still with her, things going south but she ain't going nowhere." Money replied.

Money never really understood his father's attachment with Lauren but he had a big one. On the night Money brought her to his parents' home to meet them, Jerry told Money to stay with her. Jerry knew Money would fall for Lauren but he also knew the loyalty Money had for him and his business that eventually he would stick to his plan. Money didn't always agree with his father but that was his father and he would never question him or betray him.

He arrived at the spot and Troy pulled up right behind him. "What's good, my dude?" Money asked. Upset and ready to fight, Troy told him about a rival gang from across town that hit up one of Money's traps for a few grand and killed Tommy, one of his boys. They knew who was involved and already had the boys put a hit out on them. Money wasn't letting up on anybody and he didn't care who was in the way. Once Money knew the plan, he dapped Troy up; they said their goodbyes and split ways. Money dreamed of getting out of that street life for his safety, but the money turned him into a monster and he knew it wasn't going to happen anytime soon.

Money arrived home and walked into the house with the lights dimmed and saw a freshly cooked meal on the table waiting for him. He didn't see Lauren until he walked into his bedroom to find her sound asleep. He stood in the doorway and stared at her for a while. He felt he was in love with the enemy and he was so confused about why his father wanted him to be with her. When they first started dating, he made sure to treat her like the queen she was, but one day, things changed suddenly. At the slightest mistake she would make, he would get extremely angry with her and soon he began beating on her.

His whole attitude toward her shifted and he had no idea why. He felt that cheating on her would help him keep his sanity because he questioned whether she was who he was supposed to be with. The night they met, he knew he wanted no one else but now he couldn't stop thinking about why his father needed him to stay with her. It was puzzling to him as he began thinking about the things he had done to her.

He shook his head to clear his thoughts and went into the dining room to eat the dinner Lauren had prepared for him. After taking his shower and putting on his boxers, Money climbed into bed with Lauren. He kissed her on her neck and she woke up. She felt like this would be a good time to tell him about losing her job because he seemed to be in an okay mood. She explained what had happened and he just sighed. The room became silent while Money was in deep thought.

Lauren was afraid of what he was going to do next. She laid in the dark for a few minutes worried about whether she was going to have to guard her stomach but she eventually heard Money snoring. She let out a huge sigh of relief. She didn't want to tell him about the baby now because she figured it would be a little too much to announce at one time; so she kept it to herself until she knew it was the right time.

She scooted back just a little so she could tuck herself up under him and as she dozed back off to sleep, she wished this moment where everything was calm, cool and collected could last forever.

Chapter 4

One month later.

Lauren sat in the waiting room of the women's choice clinic. She was the third woman in line to get checked in. While filling out the paperwork, the office door opened and she grew more nervous as the nurse came out. She felt she should've told someone what was going on so she could get this weight off of her shoulders but she wanted to be sure that she was going to keep the baby.

She knew her family would be happy but it would be a huge disappointment because Money was the child's father and because they weren't married. It was already bad enough that she was having sex before marriage. On her 18th birthday, Money took her out to celebrate and then moved her out of her parent's house the next day.

The nurse finally called Lauren's name to come into the back room. Her adrenaline immediately started rushing. She wished she would've at least told one person so someone could be here with her for support. As the nurse's assistant checked her vitals, Lauren tried to calm herself down. "Is this your first pregnancy sweetie?" the assistant asked.

"Yes ma'am." Lauren replied

"I can tell. Just take a few deep breaths and relax."

"I'm trying to ma'am. I'm just so nervous. I don't know what to expect."

"That's understandable. It will be okay. The nurse will be in shortly. Would you like some water while you wait?" the assistant asked

"No thank you." Lauren responded

"Okay. It'll be just a few more minutes."

The door opens, "Hello, Ms. Jacobs, my name is Julia Wilson and I'll be your nurse throughout your pregnancy. Is this your first pregnancy?"

"Yes" replied Lauren.

Mrs. Wilson could feel the tension and started to comfort her about her pregnancy. When she noticed Lauren's look, she handed her a brochure for the abortion clinic around the corner.

"I apologize Mrs. Wilson. I'm extremely nervous and scared. Something is telling me to keep this baby but I don't know if I should. I don't believe in getting an abortion but I do have a million thoughts running through my mind about this pregnancy, because I don't think I could result to giving the child up either."

"I understand you're a first-time mother and things can be hard but I promise you, it will get better. There are plenty of programs for pregnant women. Assistance is available if you need financial help, as well as, other options for clothing, food, etc." responded Mrs. Wilson.

Lauren remained quiet as she was in deep thought. Mrs. Wilson asked questions about her health and told everything important thing she needed to know to keep healthy during her pregnancy.

"Lauren, you're 9 weeks pregnant which means you'll be in your second trimester soon. Do you want to hear your babies heartbeat?" Mrs. Wilson asked.

Lauren nodded her head yes as she headed over to get the heart monitor from the cabinet. Lauren lay back on the table and unzipped her pants while waiting on her.

"Okay, this gel is going to be a little cold on your stomach at first, so just be prepared. It will get warm once I rub it in well.

Mrs. Wilson rubbed the monitor handle onto Lauren's stomach to find the heartbeat and once she heard the thud through the speakers, Lauren gasped. She couldn't believe she was actually hearing her child's heartbeat.

"Oh, my God. This is amazing." Lauren blurted out.

She couldn't describe the feeling that came over her but all she could feel was a sense of peace and it instantly calmed her down. She had never felt this feeling before and it left her speechless.

-Money

"Baby, grab me a soda out of the store." Samantha said to Money. Money never went anywhere with Samantha. She was just someone he was smashing but when he went to her place, she didn't have any more blunts. As he was leaving her house to go to the corner store, Samantha grabbed her purse and ran behind him.

They pulled up to the store and as Money got out of the car, he spotted a dude who had on a hoodie standing on the corner looking around. He didn't think anything of it because for him that was normal. As he walked into the store, the guy followed behind him. Money got what he needed and went to the counter to pay. When he finished paying, he turned to go outside and the guy hit him across the head with a bottle.

"Yeah nigga, we about take over!" he yelled.

Money grabbed his head and fell to the floor. His vision blurred for a few seconds. As soon as the man started to run outside, Money gained focus, pulled his pistol from his holder, and shot him in the leg. The man stopped dead in his tracks, bent down and grabbed his leg. He knew he had been hit but still tried to run out of the store.

The man began to lose speed. He tripped and eventually fell on his back. The store clerk was frantic when she heard the bottle break. Once the gun shot went off, it was utter chaos. A woman and her child were screaming and the clerk was yelling for the men to get out of his store. All Money cared about at that moment was blood. As he stood up and walked over to the guy, he asked the man, "Who sent you?" When he got close enough to take a good look, he was stunned by who he saw.

Money couldn't believe what was going on and he had fire in his eyes ready to kill. The guy looked Money in his face but didn't say a word. Money wasn't playing any games and wanted him to be an example to whomever sent him to do his dirty work, so he shot him twice in the face. "Yeah nigga, you thought you were taking over. You thought wrong."

After shooting the guy, he heard gunshots firing outside. In a state of shock and confusion, Money ran into an aisle to take cover. The clerk ducked behind the counter trying not to get caught in the cross fire and called the police.

When the shots stopped, Money got up and ran toward the front of the store. Looking out the window, he noticed his car was shot up. He ran outside in a panic because he forgot Samantha had been outside waiting for him. All Money could do was drop his head once he got around to the passenger side of the car. He hung his head after he saw a huge bullet hole pierced through her chest and on the side of her head.

Samantha was lying over on her door and Money didn't know what to do. He knew instantly that Samantha was gone. He started to feel bad knowing that she was caught in the middle of his rival's attack on him. She was innocent. He didn't know how he would explain everything to Lauren. All kinds of thoughts entered his mind because he knew that the word would get out about Samantha tagging along with him. Lauren thought Samantha and Money barely knew each other and Lauren never brought Samantha around him because she didn't trust her mainly because she knew how Samantha was with other females and their men.

Money grabbed his belongings from the car and ran down 15th street. As he ran away, he heard police sirens and the fire trucks coming nearby. He ducked down in a bush by an old abandoned home. What just happened messed him up big time. He noticed blood coming down the side of his face but he didn't feel the pain because his adrenaline had kicked. "Man, what is going on?" he said to himself. "I can't believe this, man!"

-Lauren

As Lauren was scheduling her next appointment to see Mrs. Wilson, she received a call from Starr. Lauren ignored it at first. She just wanted time to think and dwell on what she had just heard and experienced. After Starr's call, a call came in from Janae and she finally answered thinking they had to be together due to the calls coming in back to back.

"Hello" Lauren said in an aggravated tone.

"Lauren, Samantha just got shot and she's in critical condition! We're up at the hospital now. Hurry up!" Janae screamed in the phone.

As Lauren arrived at the hospital, she was quickly greeted by Janae, Starr, and Samantha's older cousin, Tracey. Samantha's mother and father hadn't arrived yet.

"What happened?" Lauren asked with tears running down her face.

"Samantha got shot twice at that corner store on 19th Street" Starr replied.

"Who did it? Was it females? I'm so confused. What was she even doing at that ghetto behind store?" Lauren asked.

"We have no clue but let's just pray she'll be okay." Janae mentioned. Janae pulled up her bible app on her phone and started to pray while everyone else took seats. They all were anxiously waiting for the doctor to come out so he could tell them how Samantha was and when they would let them back to see her.

Moments later, a doctor came out and introduced himself as Dr. Chapman. "Hello, are you all family?" he asked.

Starr quickly replied with a yes because she wasn't sure if he would tell them anything if they weren't.

"Alright well, I'm extremely sorry to announce this but Ms. Jones didn't make it. We tried everything that we could but we were unsuccessful. She was deceased at the scene." Dr. Chapman said softly.

Starr screamed while the others burst out crying. "I can't believe what I'm hearing right now. Too much been going on and now this? Why?"

As Janae tried to calm Starr and Samantha's cousin down, Lauren walked away to clean her face and get a breath of fresh air. She was shocked and hurt. As she walked out of the hospital through the emergency room exit, two police men were walking in. Lauren felt the urge to turn around so that she could see what was going on. She wanted to know whether it was about her friend or not. She walked by the restrooms to the water fountain. She wanted to get close enough to where the police were so she could hear their conversation with the nurse.

"Yeah, we got a call about a shooting inside the store. When we arrived on scene, we saw a male's body inside the store and a woman's body inside a black vehicle. Both were DOA."

When Lauren heard the police giving a description of the scene to their captain and the nurse, she began to wonder who the male was on the inside of the store. "We've identified the male as Troy Johnson and the female as Samantha Jones. We are currently looking for a man identified as Travis Williams."

Lauren almost fainted. She couldn't accept what she was hearing. She needed to figure out why Money would kill his best friend and why Samantha was in Money's car. Lauren's eyes filled with tears even more as she tried her best not to scream. The nurse took notes and collected all the information she could about this case.

"Troy Johnson was known to be one of Mr. Williams' best friends. One of our informants stated that a rival gang robbed Mr. Williams and his gang at one of his drug houses. Word on the street is that Mr. Johnson was behind the whole thing because of jealousy. We aren't sure if Ms. Jones is a girlfriend, a friend, or a prostitute but we're furthering our investigation." said one of the policemen.

Lauren started crying uncontrollably and caught the police's attention. She was baffled and didn't know who to turn to or what to do.

Ten minutes later, Lauren's phone rang again. As she cleaned up her face and was about to walk back to where her friends and sister were, she answered the phone. It was Money calling.

"Hello" Lauren answered. "Listen Lauren, something went down and I won't be home for a few months. I have about 30 G in the safe to cover expenses while I'm gone. I can't talk about it right now but I'm about to get rid of this phone." Lauren was already crying. "but babe how will I speak to you? I can't stay in that place alone, not at this time, I need you."

Lauren had so many questions to ask about what happened that she couldn't control herself. It was definitely bad timing to tell him anything about their child so she just kept quiet. "Money, I have no clue what happened but how did Samantha end up dead in your car?" Lauren asked.

"Man, I don't have time to explain that! I'm trying to help you out by making sure you're good while I'm gone. I can't tell you my next location but I'll be in touch with you whenever I feel the time is right. I have too much on my plate right now." Money said.

Lauren's phone hung up and all she could think about was what was going to be her next move. She could feel that something bad was going down and she didn't want to hear anything about it. She's pregnant, jobless, man less, and will be homeless if this cash that Money left runs out.

Chapter 5

Money's been ducking and dodging out at his father's house for the past two weeks. He still hasn't called Lauren but she did run across his mind. He would've called her sooner but he was concerned about how he was going to explain the situation with Samantha getting killed in his car. The one time he chose to let her ride with him, some mess pops off and she gets caught in the cross fire. He had to think of something because he knew she was going to ask him about it again when he got in contact with her.

He was stressing like a mad man, not just about Lauren but about the fact that he had a lot of heat on his back. The episode that happened at the corner store hurt him to his core. "This nigga Troy was supposed to be my right hand man." Money said under his breath in disbelief.

"I can't believe I had to take out my own. Now, I wonder if he was the reason my stacks ain't been moving the way they're supposed to." he questioned within himself.

His army was in hiding too. The cops had an informant in every gang and with the way the cops had been hanging around in the street, lately, nobody was safe.

Money was always welcomed at his parents' house but when he wasn't bringing any money through, it was a problem for them.

"Aight Trav, how you let your right hand man play you?" asked Jerry.

"Man, Pops, everything was good with me and this nigga. We met at the spot and chopped it up about getting revenge on these clowns that robbed me. Come to find out, Troy was behind the whole thing!"

"And how you figured that?" questioned Jerry.

"Because the streets talk and I spoke to one of my boys before I threw my phone out."

Money became more frustrated as he told the story.

"And then this dude had the audacity to try and off me with a bottle in the store. When I hit the floor and came to, I walked over to him and when he looked up at me, I couldn't believe it was him. He looked scared for his life because he knew I had no choice but to pop him and I did, twice in the face."

Jerry stared at his son's scar on his head. All he could do was shake his head because his son never got caught slipping. For it to be with a jit that he grew up with, he was ready to off something himself.

"So, since you going to be at my crib for a while, what's going to happen to your chick?" Jerry asked Money with a try me look on his face.

"Well, I told her where I stashed $30,000 for her to use and I told her that we wouldn't talk for a while."

"Nah son, I need for you to get back to her because y'all have some unfinished business." Jerry said irritated with Money.

"Pops, you know I have never questioned anything you've had to do but what's up with you and her? How do you know her and why do you keep worrying about her, man, because it's starting to get to me?"

Jerry looked off as he thought about some of the skeletons in his closet that would soon fall out, so he kept it brief with Money.

"Travis, I have an issue with her people, I want to get to them through her. I need you to keep her close but don't fall in love with the trick." Jerry said.

"Well, now I'm stuck between a rock and a hard place because when I brought her to meet y'all, I didn't bring her knowing you wanted her people's head. I brought her because she was who I wanted to commit to. Now, I'm treating her like a dog and I've already smashed half of the city behind her back because of some issues you have with her people. Man that's jacked up!" Money stressed to his father.

"Just find a way to get back to her. I know it's hot in these streets but I don't need you in my house when I need you with her." Jerry said as he stared into Money's eyes to see where his head was at. Money had a blank stare and left the situation alone.

–Lauren

A text came in that said, "God has a strong anointing on your life baby. I know you're going through a lot and you won't talk to me about it but talk to God before it's too late."

Lauren, confused, looked at the text and wondered why her mom texted her out of the blue. Lauren had a few things she needed to figure out, so she opted not to text her back. Lauren needed to pay some bills so when she arrived at her apartment; she went to where Money said the stash would be. He told her the stash was in a safe box behind the wall in their closet but when she got there, the money was gone.

She began to panic. "I remember him clearly saying the stash would be here! Where is it?" She tore up everything in the closet searching for the money but didn't find anything. "The only ones who knew about this was me, Money, and Troy. There's no way Money would leave me, tell me the stash was here and the stash not be here. I don't believe this!"

She sat on the bed crying, "Troy had to have come in here one evening while we were gone. He was supposed to be Money's best friend. I can't believe he would come into our home and take all of the money Travis had stashed away for me!"

Lauren grew stressed like never before because she was now officially broke with only nine hundred dollars to her name. It was all she had in her purse and that wasn't even half of the expenses she had to pay for the month. "Man, I'm getting sick of this! If it ain't one thing it's another."

Lauren was now in her second trimester and still no one knew she was pregnant. Everything was starting to take a toll on her. Starr called to check up on Lauren and Lauren told her everything that had been going on except about the pregnancy. Starr suggested coming over so she could keep her company. Lauren was cool with that because she needed someone to talk to right about now.

When Starr arrived, the police arrived a few minutes later.

"Hello, is this Lauren Jacob's and Travis William's residence?" the officer asked.

Lauren responded, "Yes. May I help you?"

"Is Mr. Williams here by chance?"

"No he isn't. Is there something I can help you with?" Lauren said shaking with fear. She didn't know what to do or how to respond to the cops.

"We will need you to get your belongings and evacuate the premises. We are closing this apartment for evidence in a double homicide case that we believe Mr. Williams was involved with." the second officer said.

Starr didn't waste any time. She grabbed Lauren's arms and helped her grab whatever they could fit in their hands.

"Starr what am I gonna do? Where am I gonna go?" Lauren said as she started to cry again.

"It's okay, you can come to my place and we will figure out the next step. For now, we have to get out of these cops' face." Starr said as she hurried to grab her purse and keys. Lauren and Starr left the condo and went to Starr's place.

Lauren woke up to a call from her sister, Janae. She insisted on coming over so she could pray for her after hearing what had happened from Starr. Lauren told her to come but she was really aggravated. Her whole body was aching having to sleep on Starr's couch and she woke up nauseous. The baby was starting to get the best of her and she felt she wouldn't be able to hide it too much longer.

Thirty minutes hadn't even passed and Janae arrived at Starr's apartment.

"Hey sis, how you been?" Janae asked while giving Lauren a huge hug.

"I've been okay just trying to cope with everything, you know."

"Mama has been asking about you. She said you haven't been answering her calls or texts. Daddy has been worried sick about you too"

"I know but they just want to pray about everything when we do talk. I just need something different. Like, I need something to be placed into action right now before I start cutting tricks and slinging crack around here."

"I understand, Lauren, but you don't think that in this time of need you should at least say a prayer? God isn't the one harming you; it's nobody but the devil." Janae explained.

"Okay, but God is the one allowing it to happen." Lauren said.

"Yes, only because he is trying to get your attention. He wants you to come to him. You're acting as though you don't believe in him at all, Lauren, and you know he's real. You know he is here for you but you're ignoring it because of worldly reasons. STOP IT!" Janae screamed growing more frustrated with her sister.

Lauren acted as if everything she's gotten and everything she's been brought through isn't of God. Janae's relationship with the Lord became stronger as she started realizing the dreams and visions he was giving to her. She and Lauren both experienced dreams since they were younger but Janae took it more seriously. Lauren always brushed everything off, even when she received signs. Janae knows the power of the Lord and she wanted to make her sister realize it as well. Lauren became silent. As she was in deep thought she said, "Okay sis, let's calm down."

"What's your next step?" Janae asked.

"Honestly, I have no idea but I have to find a quick come up. I need to find out what's up with me and Travis and also..." Lauren went silent again.

Janae looking at Lauren puzzled as to why she suddenly stopped talking. "What, Lauren and also, what?" Janae asked

"And also figure out what I'm going to do with my baby." Lauren replied hesitantly.

"WHAT? Lauren, you're pregnant? When were you going to tell me?"

"I've just had a lot on my mind. I don't want to speak about it right now."

Janae was excited for her sister and at the fact that she was going to be a new auntie, but she became sad because of everything going on with Lauren. She didn't want anything or anyone to harm her sister or the baby so she immediately began praying silently for them as Lauren went to greet Starr.

"Hey y'all, what's up?" Starr said as she entered her apartment. Starr had to run out to grab a few personal items, an air mattress for Lauren, and some more groceries.

"Aww Starr you didn't have to do that. I was okay with sleeping on the couch or the floor." Lauren said.

"Nah you're my girl. I can't have you sleeping that way. It's bad enough you're in the living room. I wish I had a guest bedroom for you." Starr replied.

"Thank you my friend!" Lauren smiled as she felt somewhat relieved because her body was sore.

"Alright ladies, I have to head out and run a few errands. You two be good while I'm gone." Janae said sternly with a smile as she gave her girl and her sister a kiss on the cheek.

"You know we're always good." laughed Starr as they said their goodbyes and she locked the door behind Janae.

Starr prepared a nice hot meal for herself and Lauren and sat with her on the couch to watch a movie.

"Starr, I have something to tell you. I want to apologize beforehand for keeping it from you because you're my girl and we're close." Lauren said.

Starr was sitting patiently and quietly, waiting for her to come clean about whatever was going on because she had a few things to fill her in about as well.

"Well, first, I need that connect you got at work because I need to start moving some." Lauren said as Starr's eyes grew wide.

"Who, Chico? Lauren, are you serious? Do you think you know enough to get mixed up into all of that? I know you're in a bad position right now but you don't have to go down that route."

"Starr, can you please just hit him up so I can get plugged in. I need it. I'm knowledgeable and I'm grown." Lauren affirmed Starr she would be okay.

Money isn't around anymore and I obviously don't have another source of income so I need this right now, just for a little bit." Lauren said.

"Alright girl but even though I have a job, I have to be in on it with you. I can't let you go through this alone. We riding through this together and that's that."

"Okay Starr. That's fine. Oh and another thing...I'm 11 weeks pregnant."

"What? Since when, and you just asked me to plug you in with work. Are you out of your mind?" Starr jumped on the couch with Lauren to rub her stomach.

"I'm not that far along, I have to make moves before I get huge. I need money not for myself but to stack bread for my baby too."

"Okay Lauren, I'm so happy for you! I can't wait to be an auntie! I really don't think you should do this but I know I can't stop you but best believe that I'll beat your behind if you start showing and you still trying to hustle. You can stay with me for as long as you need. I'll contact Chico so we can get our paper up then that's it, right?"

"Fa sho, I wouldn't have it any other way, and I want to thank you for allowing me to stay at your place for a while. Man, I can't believe I don't have anything and then I'm pregnant on top of it all."

"You'll be just fine, Lauren. You're my chick for life. Never forget that." Starr smiled as she gave Lauren a hug. They watched movies and made future plans for Lauren and Money's baby before heading to bed for the night.

Chapter 6

Starr and Lauren have been out shopping all morning for prenatal vitamins, female hygiene supplies and for panties. Lauren was conscious of the money she was spending because she didn't have much of it left and really needed it to stretch for a while. She was still in shock about the stashed cash. Having that money would really help her and her baby but she fought to keep her mind off of everything bad that was going on in her life right now, so she enjoyed the moment with her friend.

As they walked through the stores and Lauren noticed all the couples out shopping, it made her miss being with Money. He was on her mind day and night and she was curious to know where he was staying or whom he was laying up with. She tried not to let that stress her out but the thoughts would always creep back up on her. She knew she was his ride or die chick but she didn't understand why she couldn't hide out with him. She didn't want to be alone, especially now that she was pregnant and she was willing to take on the world with him if only he would let her.

Starr interrupted Lauren's daydream, "Hey Lauren, I called Chico up and he told us to drop through his spot around 9 tonight. Are you still down?"

"Umm yeah chick, I got to get this money. I have no choice and I ain't going to my parents for anything. I've been meaning to ask you though, what was it that you needed to talk to me about last night?" Lauren asked.

Starr instantly felt guilty knowing what went on between Samantha and Money and now she's dead over it. "Come on, let's go get in the car." Starr replied.

As they headed toward the car, Lauren started feeling a sense of nervousness and confusion and she was starting to get hot on the inside. She couldn't describe what was going on because she had never experienced this before and it wasn't normal for her. She just wanted to sit down.

As they got settled in the car, Starr took a deep breath.

"Alright, I love you Lauren but I honestly don't think you could bare what I'm about to tell you." Starr said with shakiness in her voice.

"Just tell me please." Lauren responded.

"Okay Lauren, I don't know how to say this, but I found out that Samantha and Money were messing around for a while before she was killed. One day, I was chilling over Samantha's house when Money texted her. He then called her after a few minutes when she didn't respond. She was in the shower when the text and the call came through so I was able to see his name. I was confused because I thought he didn't fool with Samantha like that but then I became concerned because I thought something had happened to you. That's the reason I called you in a panic a while back. I didn't tell you then because I didn't want you to get upset if what I was thinking wasn't really true. I needed to make sure first."

As Starr explained everything to Lauren that she had learned from Samantha that day, Lauren grew extremely angry. At that moment, she was happy Money was in hiding so she wouldn't be in jail for murder and she had the evil thought in the back of her mind that she was glad Samantha was already dead. "She's been messing with my man, my child's father? I can't even think straight!" Lauren said.

Starr figured they would leave the store and she would go ahead and take Lauren back to her apartment so she could rest before their meet up with Chico tonight. Their minds had to be focused and in the game if Chico was going to even consider working with them. On the ride back to Starr's apartment, Starr kept quiet allowing Lauren to vent her anger and frustrations. There was no way for her to help the situation any further so she encouraged her to calm down and relax, especially for the sake of the baby.

Lauren became weak and her vision started getting blurry. After venting to Starr, she took a deep breath and tried her best to calm down for the sake of her sanity and for her baby because the way she felt now, she could kill Samantha two more times and throw Money's body in the hole with her.

They arrived at Starr's apartment and Lauren headed straight to the bathroom.

"I'm going to take a little nap before tonight, Starr, is that okay with you?" asked Lauren.

"Yes, go right ahead. We had a long day today and I know you have a lot on your mind that you need to sleep on. Get you some rest. I don't plan on going anywhere anyway."

It was almost nine o'clock and the girls were on their way to meet with Chico. After a good nap and still in her feelings, Lauren remained quiet the entire trip. Starr was still thinking about the news she had to share with her friend earlier. She was also nervous about what they were getting themselves into with Chico. Lauren was adamant about stacking her paper before her pregnancy began to show and even though she didn't want Lauren involved with Chico, she definitely wasn't going to let her do it alone.

As they pulled up to Chico's spot and got out of the car to go inside, one of Chico's goons greeted the girls at the door. His eyes were full of lust, staring at them like they were a piece of meat ready for dinner and he would've taken full advantage if he could. This was business so he kept his composure.

Lauren and Starr didn't look like they should be coming here but they did look like they were about their business. Lauren came through the spot with her black red bottom Christian Louboutin heels, a black high waist skirt, and one of her favorite cream blouses. She didn't look a day pregnant in her fit and she wanted to keep it that way for as long as she could. Starr rocked her favorite Chanel shades, a black one piece and her leather Gucci heels. They strutted through Chico's place looking like a bag of money and they were the boss.

They walked up focused and ready to show Chico that they were the official bad chicks and that he needed them to be on his team. With their sexy looks and the street knowledge they carried, he would see they were profitable. Chico's goons hounded the girls as they made their way to Chico's office. Lauren wasn't a bit of nervous. She felt she was built for this but her man was too overprotective and never let her in the game with him.

When they got to the office door, one of Chico's doormen held out his left hand motioning the girls to stop and put his right hand on the gun in his belt.

"What's your business?" he said with a stern voice.

Lauren looked him up and down crossing her arms while Starr explained, "We have a meeting with Chico. Tell him Starr and Lauren are here."

He went into Chico's office and closed the door behind him. A few moments later, he opened the door wide enough for both Lauren and Starr to walk through. As they walked into the office, both men at the door watched them as their plump rumps moved side to side. The doorman then closed the door behind them.

As they got closer to Chico's desk, Lauren and Starr helped themselves to a seat. Chico was turned around counting his money on the money machine and paid them no mind until he was finished with his last stack. When he turned toward them, he looked ready for business. He wasn't pressed by their attire but he did think that they looked fly. He was ready to talk numbers and then he could figure out which one he wanted to smash later.

"What's up?" Starr asked.

"Start talking." Chico said with a deep Dennis Haysbert voice that surprisingly turned both the girls on.

"Me and my girl are trying to get some money so we want to help move some of your weight. We're book and street smart and understand the game. The police first target wouldn't be a female so we're sure we could hide the work." Starr said.

Chico stared at them both, rubbing his chin in deep thought. He was strong and ran a heavy business. He had his goons on every block and they were always ready to knock anyone off to be on top. Chico stood 5'10 with gorgeous brownish green eyes, curly hair and a small goatee that he kept sharp and clean. He had on a few platinum chains and some nice kicks but he kept it simple because he didn't want to make himself a distraction or a target, so he mainly wore a t-shirt and some plain Levi's. His skin was as red as clay and he was tatted from his neck to his ankles. He was extremely attractive but the girls didn't want to go any further with him than doing business.

At least that was Lauren's plan even though Money had stepped out on her with her friend.

After thinking for a minute, "Alright ladies, I'm going to start you off small and see what you can do within 3 days and we will go from there. If y'all mess me over I don't mind putting a bullet in a female head because this is my business. I don't care how good y'all look." Chico said as his two guards showed their guns and Chico pulled his blunt.

"Okay bet. We got you. You'll see." Starr said as she and Lauren grabbed the bag with the product and started out the door.

Staying a little behind Starr, Lauren looked back at Chico and said "Hand me a piece."

Chico looked at Lauren in confusion because this was the first thing she's said since being in the room. "What you mean give you a piece? You don't run this , you ask me Shorty."

Lauren looked him square in the eye "I said hand me a piece. I ain't trying to protect myself. I'm trying to protect your product. You being a business man should understand and supply."

Chico went in his desk and grabbed her a nine. He had plenty of guns and giving her one wasn't an issue. His issue was how she said it and how she questioned his intelligence on his business. It made him speechless but he was intrigued by her. As she turned to walk out the office, he checked her up and down. He never laid eyes on a woman like this before. She didn't have to say she was a boss. She owned it and carried herself like one. Her sassiness and confidence made him attracted to her. He never dealt with a woman like this and the more he checked her out, the more he wanted Lauren to be his Bonnie.

Lauren was mad at Money but was still his ride or die. She had no intention of switching up on him right now. As the girls got in their car and left, Chico stood by his desk talking to one of his boys about them. One of his goons busted in his office with a confused look "Bruh, you know that punk Money that we hit up with Troy? That's his girl who just walked out of here. I passed her and mean mugged her in the hallway but she didn't look my way. What she doing here?"

Chico looked nervous wondering what he had just gotten himself into. His location was exposed, he gave his work to these females and now they've seen his face. He thought Lauren and Starr were trying to hit a lick on him but then again, he didn't want to make any unnecessary moves until he monitored what was going on.

"Those are my new girls but whatever they got going on, I promise you, they won't get far. Word on the street is that Money is ducking but if he sent his girl then I'm on both of them. For now, I'm going to play this game to see how things play out."

Chico should've known that something was up with Lauren because of her high priced clothing and the way in which she carried herself. He was attracted to the enemy's trick and wasn't sure if he should be aware or take advantage of the situation. He needed time to think things over but he knew one thing, nobody was going to mess him over. He was ready for whatever popped off.

A week later, Starr found herself in a crazy position. Down on her knees in a hotel room, she felt the attraction between them two but he also made her feel used. She hadn't been intimate with anyone in a few months and she felt she needed to spice things up. She was getting bored with her sex life and she wanted more excitement.

When she was done with Chico, he got out of the bed and walked to the bathroom. Starr sat up on the bed wanting to have a conversation. She wanted some quality time but she felt weird and confused by the way he stood up and walked away. He made her feel dirty. She waited for Chico to clean himself up and hoped he would come back to lay with her.

"Chico are you okay in there?"

"Yeah man, come here!" Chico yelled out the bathroom door.

As Starr got close to the bathroom, she wondered why he would call her in there but then she thought that maybe he wanted a round two. She opened the bathroom door and saw a line of coke on the counter. Chico held his head back as he wiped his nose from the sniff he had just taken. He had an ongoing supply of the product and didn't see a problem testing for quality control.

Starr came in the bathroom and sat on the toilet as she watched Chico getting high. She was too nervous to ask why he had called her in there so she remained quiet.

"Hit this line." Chico told Starr.

Her heart started beating almost out of her chest. She was scared. She had never done anything like this before and was never around anyone else doing it. Snorting coke and selling it were two different things. As she sat stunned thinking about what he had just told her to do, Chico became enraged and smacked her so hard she fell off the toilet onto the floor. He grabbed her hair and pulled her up off the floor. He pushed her head to the sink so she could snort the line.

"Trick didn't I tell you to hit this? What's taking you so long? Don't make me repeat myself!" he yelled in her face with his hand tangled around her hair.

Starr caught her balance and held onto her hair in Chico's hand, with her face flooded with tears, she snorted the line. Her life flashed before her eyes. "How did I get in this place? I've never been treated like this before. What is going on?" She thought quietly as the drug penetrated her nostrils.

Chico didn't mind putting his hands on Starr because he only saw her as a piece of meat. He thought she was attractive but her conversation told him that she wasn't someone he could take seriously, and until he figured out what was going on with this Lauren and Money situation, she would be the only one he would consider adding to his team.

It didn't take long for Starr to feel the effects of the coke. She was so high; all she could do was sit in the corner on the bathroom floor. Still crying from the blow Chico laid on her, she wiped the blood running from her nose. After about ten minutes, Starr got up, ran a hot shower and cleaned herself up.

Chico got all his things from the room and left while she was in the shower. She wanted to talk to someone about what just happened but she was too afraid and embarrassed to say anything. She knew Lauren would question her about the bruise whenever she saw her face so she definitely didn't want to face her right now. She didn't want anyone to know she had just been beaten up by Chico. She also didn't want Lauren to know that she had slept with him and he made her do his drugs.

She got out of the shower and listened to hear if Chico was still in the room. She poked her head out of the bathroom door and noticed he had left. She was relieved because she didn't know what else he was capable of doing. She came out of the bathroom, put on her clothes and laid down. She lay on her back facing the ceiling with her mind going 100 miles a minute, and thought "After this, how could I face the world?"

-Lauren

Moving that dope seemed like nothing to Lauren. She built up her clientele and was doing the doggone thang. Lauren didn't have to stand on the block. She knew the boys from around the way. The niggas that tried to step to her when she went out somewhere, brought from her after she ran a little talk game. Lauren was banking and Chico and his team loved it. Starr was also doing her thing but wasn't making much of an impression on his team like Lauren.

Lauren noticed Starr never talked as much as she used to anymore. She thought it was strange but didn't pay it any mind because things were going good. She had no clue what happened between Starr and Chico because everything seemed normal between the two. Chico remained himself and acted as if nothing happened between him and Starr. His team got used to having female hustlers on their side.

They had their backs but of course they also tried to get them on their back from time to time. Lauren stood her ground with all of them. She was about her stacks. Chico was the only one who Starr gave the time of day to. Lauren felt at peace now with more money coming in, but she knew the hustle would end sooner or later because of her pregnancy. She wanted to say forget it and get an abortion so she could keep banking but something kept telling her to not do it.

She opened a bank account and started saving while helping Starr with a few of her expenses around her house. She wanted to show her gratitude for letting her crash there until she could get on her feet. Lauren was making enough money to move into her own place and to be able to keep up with expenses but she figured staying with Starr would help her save more money in the meantime. Starr wasn't a hard person to live with nor did she complain about her getting out.

Lauren had no desire to look for another job because the money she was making working with Chico was way more than what she would make in a month on a regular nine to five. She never knew why Money kept her from this life when it wasn't as hard as he made it look. They could have taken over the streets together bringing in double the profit but he wanted her to look legit so she could be the cover for his money. Lauren felt powerful and super bad living this hustle life. She was the baddest chick on her block. She was living the life she imagined when she was young a girl.

Chico kept his cool even though he knew Lauren was Money's girl. With the way she was working on his team, it made him hold off on killing her. Chico made sure none of his goons knew anything about her and Money because they would've offed her on their own. He knew his goons would react if his life was threatened or if they thought something was going down so he kept it between a select few just so they would keep an eye out.

It was time for Lauren and Starr to re-up again but Starr decided to sit this one out. She was still upset with Chico from the night he beat her. Lauren didn't think anything strange about it because Starr had done it before. When Lauren got to Chico's spot she stepped out with some leather brown boots, high waist pants and a leather brown jacket. Her hair was pinned up nice and her make-up was done.

Lauren and Starr had plans to go to dinner and chat after they handled their business since it had been a while for them hanging out.

"Yoo Chico, I'm here for my re-up!" Lauren said as she walked in his office.

Chico sat there looking as fine as ever as he got up to grab a bag from the safe.

"I got you ma. You know you one of my best sellers right now. Maybe one day you can run this empire with me." Chico smiled giving Lauren the sexy eyes.

Lauren was super attracted to Chico but she didn't want to cross boundaries. Chico walked over to her, put his hand on her back and kissed her neck. Lauren let him continue for a moment and then she hesitantly stopped him.

"Chico what are you doing?" she asked.

"What it look like? I want you in every way possible." He said still kissing on her. He tried to be gentle with her.

"I'm involved with someone. I don't need any extra baggage in my life and I want to keep everything strictly business between us."

Chico became angry "I'm the plug, who turns down the plug?"

"Obviously you don't get turned down much but I'm the one to turn down the plug. I don't need you for anything other than to be my plug."

Chico couldn't believe what he was hearing. It made his wheels start turning all the more. Was she there to set him up? Lauren had no clue Chico and his goons were the ones who tried to kill Money with the help of Troy or that they were the ones to kill Samantha. She was on a money making mission and even though she knew about the streets, she didn't know a thing about the beef.

Chapter 7

"Why haven't you been answering your phone, Lauren?" Janae asked, aggravated with her sister. Janae and her mom have been blowing up Lauren's phone with no answer for the past few weeks.

"I didn't answer my phone because I've been busy putting in overtime." Lauren replied grinning.

"What do you mean? Are you back working?"

"I mean you can say that."

"Lauren, you better not be doing anything illegal or stupid. Are you stripping or something?" Janae asked eagerly wanting to know.

"Nah but I do support that naked hustle!" Lauren laughed. "Don't worry about all that Janae, what's going on?"

"Nothing, we've just been worried about you and wanted to make sure you were okay. Have you spoken to Money yet?"

"NO, I ain't speak to that nigga yet but it's all good because he'll need me sooner than I'll need him. Believe that." Lauren replied irritated just from hearing Money's name.

Lauren had gotten so cocky that she didn't know what the word humble meant anymore. Over time, her cockiness got worse with the more money she saw coming in and out of her hands.

"Okay I guess. You should call Mom though, Lauren." Janae said.

"Yeah I'll make my way to doing so soon."

Janae sat speechless debating on what to say next. "Sister, I know what you've been doing. I can't pinpoint it but I know it isn't good and you're pregnant. You have to chill. You're going to end up in jail or even worse, dead, Lauren. I'm sorry but I don't see a great outcome from whatever you have going on. I'm just really concerned for you and your baby and no, I haven't told anyone about the baby. I know if they knew you were pregnant they would be on your tail like white on rice."

Lauren sat silently on the phone while listening to Janae and thinking about her baby. She was also tired of hearing her run her mouth so she could get off the phone. She knew she cared for her but she didn't want to hear any of that right now.

"Can I say a prayer for you, Lauren? You need it." Janae asked.

"Yes, go ahead Janae because I know you aren't getting off the phone without doing it anyway." Lauren replied.

"Father God, I pray that you cover and protect my sister from any harm that may come her way and protect that baby in her stomach. She will one day see that you are real and that she'll need you more than ever before. We appreciate you waking her up every morning and laying her down to rest peacefully through the night. I pray she has a healthy baby and a brighter future. Amen." Janae finished praying and sat silently on the phone waiting for Lauren to say Amen.

Lauren felt some type of way after Janae prayed for her. She didn't know what she was feeling but she knew that prayer was something different from the prayers she had received before. She broke the silence so she wouldn't dwell on what she was feeling so she could let her sister go. "Amen. Okay, I'm going to let you go Janae."

"Okay. Love you Lauren. Be safe." Janae replied.

"Love you too Janae. Bye."

Lauren had gone apartment hunting today and after a long day headed back to Starr's place. On her way back, she picked up a bite to eat for the both of them since groceries were running low and neither one of them wanted to cook. As Lauren walked into the apartment with her hands full of food, she called out "Starr! Come and eat! I got our favorite spot, Kim Hu's, and she added an extra egg roll for us too." Lauren laughed.

She placed the food on the kitchen table but didn't hear Starr and didn't get a reply from her. She thought maybe she had taken a nap but wanted to make sure everything was okay. Lauren checked the half bathroom in the hallway to see if the light was on. The light was off so she continued on to Starr's bedroom. She noticed the light was off in her bedroom but she saw a little twinkle of light flickering like a candle in her bathroom.

Lauren walked over to the bathroom and turned the doorknob to see if the door was unlocked. The door opened and her jaw dropped. Her eyes widened as she took a huge gasp. "STARR! WHAT ARE YOU DOING?"

"OH MY GOD, LAUREN! You don't know how to knock before you bust into someone's bathroom?" Starr yelled frantically.

"Knocking ain't the problem. Why are you in here snorting your work? How long have you been doing this?"

Starr threw a punch at Lauren and caught her in her jaw. Lauren threw a punch back and the girls began fighting. They ripped through everything in Starr's room, from the trinkets on the dresser to the radio clock on the night stand. They knocked over her clothes bin and broke a few picture frames and decorations hanging on the wall. In the midst of the fight, Lauren screamed, "Who got you into this? Man, what is going on? You've never done drugs before!"

Starr stopped hitting at Lauren and stared blankly at her. High and embarrassed, she told Lauren, "Grab your stuff and get out of my house!"

Lauren, confused, ran to the living room to pack up her things. "I can't believe you Starr! How could you do this? Who got you into using? This is not you. I just can't believe you Starr!"

Starr was the only friend Lauren felt that she had and to see her throw her life away hurt her deep to the core. As Lauren made her way to the front door, she turned around to Starr, "Starr, get you some help before you become too cracked out." Lauren turned back around and closed the door of the apartment behind her.

She left Starr's apartment and got a room at the Hilton that night. Lauren had never been so pissed in her life. To see her friend turn to using was something she would've never dreamed would happen. She would've felt better if Starr had a drink here and there or smoked a little weed every now and then but she chose to dib and dab in the hard stuff. She was smart enough to know that this is not something you try and think that you will not be hooked on. How could she do this? Lauren thought silently.

Later that night, Lauren had a meeting with Chico on some work she needed to move and it involved some traveling. After their last meeting and her turning down his advance, she didn't know how he would act this time. All she knew was that he had better be in the right state of mind and all about his business. As Lauren settled into her room and prepared to take a shower, she felt something weird in her stomach. The feeling stopped when she noticed it so she ignored it thinking it was just her imagination. She felt it again and realized she was feeling flutters from her baby.

Her mind was blown and she almost fainted with excitement. She was actually feeling her baby move and was amazed that this was actually her baby. Lauren began rubbing her stomach and started to think about all the things going on in her life. With all the thoughts she had about an abortion, she immediately began to regret even thinking about it. She didn't understand how someone would go through with one but then again, looking at some of the issues she's been facing lately would make someone wonder why she hadn't gone to the clinic herself.

Lauren wasn't sure about Money being in her baby's life but she knew she'll have much support from family. She always imagined being with someone that would be with her and only her and that she would get married and have kids. She didn't want to be anyone's baby's mama. She thought that with her being loyal to Money and no one else that she would be everything to him and more.

"I see now that things aren't going to be that way. I would be surprised if he even claimed the baby as his if he knew about it. He'll probably think I've found a new man since he's been ducking and dodging and I haven't heard from him."

Lauren snapped back to reality when she heard her phone's notification go off. Lauren jumped into the shower and got dressed for business. She pushed all feelings and thoughts aside, grabbed her gun from her duffle bag, and got ready for her meeting with her trap team.

Lauren pulled up to Chico's trap and had the strangest feeling that something wasn't right. The feeling was so strong she was debating if she should even go through with it all. She waited for a few minutes in the car, took a deep breath, and walked toward the front door. Walking through the house like normal, she got to Chico's office but Chico wasn't in there. His boys let her in, sat her down, and remained quiet by the door.

The trap usually had 20-25 dudes in and out at any given time because they were normally working the corner around this time. However, Lauren noticed that tonight there were only 4 dudes and that included Chico. As Chico walked in, she felt a strong urge to just say forget it and walk out but she sat waiting.

"What's up Lauren?" Chico said in a low tone.

To Lauren, he seemed aggravated but he was staring at his phone like something really had his attention.

"What's up? How are you feeling?"

Chico didn't reply. He continued looking at his phone and appeared to be texting. Five minutes passed and Lauren finally broke the silence.

"Alright Chico, tell me the drop spot, hand me the bag, and I'll go ahead and slide."

Chico remained quiet. He stood up and walked around his desk to where Lauren sat. He gently brushed his fingers across her hair. She felt irritated thinking he was going to try to smash again and that this time he wouldn't want to take no for an answer.

"Just please keep your hands to yourself Chico. You know we have to get this money, so where's the bag?" Lauren asked.

Chico didn't respond. He groped himself in front of her and Lauren tensed up thinking she was about to get raped from the look in his eyes. She quickly jumped out of the chair and headed for the door. Before she could reach the door, Chico grabbed her by her hair and gripped his hand around the back of her neck. Making her stumble back, Chico grew angry "Who sent you here Lauren? Was it your nigga Money? Is this his get back for us taking his right hand man?"

Lauren looked confused. She knew Chico would have known about Money because everyone knew him but she didn't think he was the one who had been beefing with him. She didn't believe he even knew she was connected to him. "No Chico, nobody sent me. What are you talking about?"

"Trick I'm about to off you if you don't come clean." Chico let her go and ran back towards his desk to grab his pistol from the drawer.

Lauren ran out of the room toward the front door only to find out that it had been bolted shut. She knew the only way she could leave through the front was if one of Chico's goons unlocked it for her. Frightened to run back toward Chico, Lauren ran and locked herself in the nearest closet in the living room. Chico knew she couldn't get out and he ran behind her but she was nowhere in sight.

"Lauren, tell me how you plan to hide in my trap. It's no way out baby girl. You might as well come out and take this bullet for your man since nobody can find him."

Lauren tried hard not to breathe loudly so she couldn't be heard. She listened to him as he walked around the house talking and laughing as he waited for her to give herself up. While she contemplated a plan of escape, she remembered that one day when she and Starr came to do business; Chico made them come through a secret back door. She remembered this door was the crew's way of escape should the police raid them. Chico knew if the police surrounded the house, they would automatically come to the front and back doors so they created a secret exit in the back of the pantry that led under the house.

Lauren heard Chico's footsteps on the hardwood floors getting closer and closer to the closet where she was hiding and she quietly stood up, determined to get her timing to break out right. She knew that if she didn't bust out at the right time she would be a dead woman. As Chico walked to the closet door and put his hand on the doorknob to open it, Lauren kicked the door open. Knocking him in the head and shattering the glass mirror all over him, he fell down on the floor screaming from the glass shards that severely cut him.

She jumped over him and made her way to the pantry and out of the secret exit. While under the house, she heard Chico running toward her direction and knew he was on her trail. She noticed a crate in the backyard near the fence, so she ran to hide under it. She wanted to make sure she was clear to get away so she lay waiting to see where he would run. She began to feel a tense sensation in her stomach and she became nervous for the baby. Rubbing her stomach to ease the tension, she figured the tension and a little pain came because of the stress from what was happening to her.

When the pressure in her stomach started to ease up, she thought the coast should be clear by now so she inched her head out from under the crate. When she looked up, Chico was standing over her with his gun pointing down to her head.

Lauren burst out crying, "Chico listen, I'm sorry! I was just trying to get money. I don't know what this beef is with you and Money but I ain't in it. I promise. I haven't even seen him. He didn't send me to you. My girl Starr knew you and we chose to come and do business with you on our own."

"Shut up trick! I knew you were Money's girl the night you and Starr came up in here. Whether he sent you or not, I still have to off you because you turned me down from smashing. It's a good thing your girl Starr didn't though and because you're Money's girl, we still looking to off that punk but getting rid of you would hurt him even more."

Lauren didn't know how to feel but her whole life flashed before her. She wanted this lifestyle. She knew it was wrong but she chose it and the environment. "Chico I'm pregnant. I just wanted to get this money for me and my jit. That's it."

"You pregnant and it's that nigga's baby? That's all the better." Chico said sarcastically. Chico cocked his gun ready to take Lauren's head off and she closed her eyes.

BOOM!

Lauren thought she was shot but didn't feel any pain and realized she was still breathing. She opened her eyes and saw Chico hit the ground next to her. As she inched out from under the crate and looked around, she saw Starr over in the corner. She hopped up and rushed over to Starr and held her tightly, crying hysterically.

"Oh my God, Starr I'm so happy to see you! Thank you so much! How did you know what was going on? Did you hear everything?" Lauren asked.

Starr didn't say anything and Lauren wasted no time trying to get her to talk. She grabbed Starr's hand and they both ran to get in her car. Lauren didn't know where Chico's goons had gone but she was extremely grateful that her friend came to her rescue even after they just had a fight.

Chapter 8

Money was still hiding out at his mom's and pop's crib. He hadn't contacted anyone yet except one of his boys from around the way. Jerry was growing frustrated with Money and Money could sense the frustration and feel the tension.

"Travis, how are you doing?" his mother asked.

"I'm good Ma, just trying to figure out my next step on this money mission."

"And what about the female you were living with, where did she go?"

"I haven't spoken to her since I've been here and to be honest, I feel bad about messing with her best friend and she ended up getting killed in the midst of a hit out on me." Money didn't care for Samantha as his woman. To him, they were just sex buddies but it still bothered him with how things went down.

Money's mother wasn't into the street life but she definitely loved the money his dad brought in. She didn't have to do much but keep Jerry happy and she stayed draped in gold with all the finest clothes.

"Travis, you know I don't fully agree with the street life. I do love the money though." she said looking at her new diamond ring. "But someday, you have to stack your bread up and retire. I don't know what I'll do if something were to happen to you. I want me, you and your father to go to church one Sunday"

"Mannnn, you know Pops not into all that and I haven't thought about it myself. I'm good though Ma."

"Whatever Travis, you'll learn about life the hard way but in the meantime, call that female friend of yours. I have a strange feeling that there's more to her than what I saw when we met. Something about her is going to make you slow down eventually." She said smiling.

Money's boy, Malcolm, called him on his prepaid phone that he purchased to check up on him and tell him what's been going on in the streets. "What's up my boy?" Malcolm said as Money answered the phone.

"Nothing much man, what's been going on?"

"These streets been real dry since you been gone; stacks ain't been rotating how they should and I have all kinds of opportunities to take back what's ours, but you niggas wanna go ducking and dodging."

"What you mean by take back what's ours? We still handling all those niggas we been beefing with and them boys still looking for me so what you mean?" Money said irritated with Malcolm's slick comment.

"Trav, Chico got killed man, the ringleader, the plug, the one who ordered his little niggas for any and every hit."

Money's mind started racing a hundred miles a second as he thought about the territories to take over and how to build his money back up. "That's what's up, who knocked him off?"

"I don't know. Nobody knows what happened. They just found him dead in the back of his trap by some crates. Hey look, I'm a hit you later man. I got a few things I need to handle. Ten four."

-Lauren

Knock, knock, knock
"Room Service"
Knock, knock, knock!
"Room Service"

Lauren woke up to a maid knocking on the door of her suite. Lauren yelled at the door "One moment please. Thank you."

Rolling over and slowly coming to, she thought about the night before after Starr showed at Chico's place. They didn't have any type of conversation as they jumped in the car and left. Lauren said thank you, they kissed cheeks and said goodbye. She had so much going through her mind about last night and she couldn't believe she was so close to losing her life. She wondered how Starr knew she was there. She was so grateful she was.

Lauren got out of bed and opened the door so the maid could do her job while she showered and prepared herself for the day. As she showered, she heard her phone ring and thought maybe it was her mother or sister. She finished up with her shower, got out and got dressed and saw that the missed the call was an unknown number. She put the phone back on the bed because she thought it might have been a bill collector or someone she just didn't want to talk to at that moment.

The same unknown number called back ten minutes later and she answered it.

"Hello"

"Hello" Money responded.

Lauren was surprised to hear Money's voice on the other end of the line. She didn't know whether she should curse him out or start crying.

"Hello?" Money responded again.

Lauren sat quietly.

"Lauren, I know you're there. Answer me."

Lauren pulled up the words to reply "Yes Travis, why are you calling my phone?"

"Because I told you I'll contact you when the time was right."

Lauren sat silently for a few seconds in deep thought. "Travis, it's been 2 months, are you serious?"

"Yes I know. Where are you at?"

"I'm in a room at the Hilton. Why does it matter?" Lauren replied.

"What you mean you're in a room at the Hilton? What happened to my apartment?"

"Well, Mr. Williams, if you had called me earlier, you would've learned that your boy Troy hit our spot and stole the stash cash before y'all had y'all incident went down and the cops came and took the apartment for evidence for their double homicide case that you were involved with." Lauren explained sarcastically.

"So, where you been staying?" asked Money.

"Well, I was at Starr's but we got into a fight and she kicked me out. Now I'm at a room."

"Come and get me, we got a lot to discuss. I'm at my parent's house."

Lauren hung up and anger rose up within her. Samantha and Money's situation kept playing over and over in her head. She wasn't sure if she wanted to leave him there or go pick him up and kill him. She was still hurt about all the things he put her through and him cheating on her with her friend. She sat contemplating everything and decided to pick him up. She wanted him to know that she was pregnant and that it was his child. She gathered her purse and keys and rolled out.

She pulled up to Money's parent's house and saw him walk out with a few bags. He put everything in the truck and jumped in the passenger seat. He looked over at Lauren and he could tell that a lot of had changed in the past two months and he could see she had a lot on her mind.

"So you ain't going to greet me with a kiss?" Money asked.

"Nah, I'm good. I'm going to take you to my room so we can talk."

Lauren drove back to the hotel in complete silence pondering how their conversation was going to go. They entered the room. Money put his bags in the corner and lay on the bed.

"I missed you Lauren"

"Pssh you don't miss nobody but Samantha"

She had never spoken to Money like that and she wasn't afraid of him right now. She was ready to fight back had he hit her. She was pissed with him even being in her presence.

"Who do you think you talking to like that?" Money huffed as he jumped off the bed. "Things really have changed since I've been gone. You don't talk to me like that."

Money wanted to swing at her but hesitated because he felt bad for messing with her best friend and her finding out about it.

"Money, I've been there for you through thick and thin. You're my first everything, I gave you my virginity, my loyalty and even put up with you hitting on me. I was never raised like that and I know I'm worth more but I decided to stay with your worthless behind" Lauren cried.

"Man, I'm sorry about Samantha. I don't know what I was thinking. She came on to me."

"Money, I knew you was going to be behind on money so I got up and started hustling." She didn't want to reveal what she had to do or make any mention of Chico.

"Who you linked up with Lauren and don't lie?" Money asked walking towards her.

Lauren put her head down and mumbled "Chico"

"What?" Money felt betrayed, pulled his gun out and put it to her head. He wasn't sure what Chico and Lauren had going on and he was two seconds from blowing her head off.

"Babe, when I went to him, I knew nothing about you beefing with him. I'm sorry." Lauren cried as she felt the gun push against her head. She knew Money loved her but she knew she could die over something like this.

"So what happened, Lauren? I heard Chico is dead now, what's really going on?" Money asked while putting his finger on the trigger.

"I don't know Travis, please put the gun down." Lauren screamed.

"You better start talking cause I'm about to shoot." He had told Lauren to stay out the streets because he knew she was curious about it since they met at the party.

"Chico found out about me being your girl. We met up so I could make a run for him but he ended up trying to kill me. When he put the gun to my head to kill me, Starr came out of nowhere and killed him."

Money pulled the gun back and stared her down. So his girl and her friend were the ones who killed the nigga he wanted dead. He was heated about her going to the enemy and working for him but he was glad he didn't have to worry about him anymore.

"Another thing Travis, I'm four months pregnant."

Money felt his heart drop as he thought about what she had just said. He paused for a minute and walked into the bathroom. Lauren got up from the floor and sat on the edge of the bed waiting for Money to come back out. She didn't know what was going to happen next. She didn't know if she needed to run out of the room while he was in the bathroom or stay to see what he was going to say. She chose to stay and when money returned from the bathroom, he walked up to her and held her close to him.

"Do you know what the baby is? Is the baby okay?" he asked as he pondered about what he had done to her. He treated her like garbage and now she was carrying his child, his only child. He made up in his mind from this day forward that he would never leave her in a messed up situation again.

Chapter 9

Eve was on her way to the grocery store to get a few things that she needed for the specialty Chicken Parmesan dinner tonight. As she drove, she thought deeply about her life and how she decided to fully give herself over to God. Her pride and joy was having her beautiful girls, Lauren and Janae. She prayed constantly for their safety and for God's guidance for them in this journey of theirs called life. She trusted that the same way God had won over Janae's heart; he would soon help Lauren to find the light as well. She raised them in the church and wanted nothing but the best for her children but she was saddened at the thought of Lauren never turning her life over to God. She noticed this attitude in her even when she was a young child but always prayed that God would soften her heart and draw her close to him. Even in all of the trials and struggles she's had to endure and watch her children go through, she still felt blessed of the Lord.

As Eve parked her car, she made her way to the store entrance. She walked passed a homeless man standing outside asking for change, so she told him that she would bring him a few waters and snacks when she came out of the store. Eve didn't believe in giving money to beggars because she would rather bless them with what they really needed like food or water in case they spent the money on something like drugs or alcohol. She would rather help with something that would sustain them. The man appeared surprised that someone would even offer to do that for him and said with excitement that he would wait for her to return and God bless.

While Eve searched for her special brand of shaved parmesan cheese, she was so focused on what she was doing that she paid no attention to whom or what was in front of her. She bumped her cart, accidently, into the back of the woman's ankles standing in front of her, in the aisle.

The woman screeched "Ouch!"

Eve apologized profusely to the lady, "I'm so sorry ma'am. I wasn't paying attention. I apologize! Are you okay?" she asked.

When the woman turned around, Eve was shocked and speechless. The woman stared into her eyes with such rage and anger that she looked as if she was ready to kill. Eve turned to walk away;

the woman grabbed a can of corn and threw it hitting Eve in the back of her head causing her right eye to black out. Eve stumbled and to catch her balance, she grabbed a hold of one of the shelves. When Eve turned to swing back at the woman, she took another blow to the face.

"Oh yeah, didn't I tell you when I see you again I'm going to kill you and I don't care where we are or who's around?" said the woman.

Eve barely able to speak shielded herself from another blow when two workers rushed over to break up the fight. One of the cashiers in the front called the police. Eve dazed by the hits could barely see what was going on around her but remembered exactly who the woman was. The workers helped her get off of the floor and she immediately ran out of the store. The employees chased her yelling "Ma'am, ma'am, we've called the police. You'll be safe now. We need you to stay for the report. Ma'am, ma'am!

Eve started her car and sped out of the parking lot like a rocket ship taking off for space. Her head spinning and not having fully regained her vision, she sped through a red stop light. As she crossed the intersection, everything went black.

"What's going on? I can't see anything. What's happening? she screamed for help but no one heard her.

"Ma'am, ma'am? Can you hear me? Are you okay?" she heard a voice a few minutes later.

"I hear you. I just don't feel good. I can't see anything. What's going on? What happened? she yelled in a panic.

"Ma'am? Can you hear me? Can you hear me? Let me know that you can hear me! Someone call 9-1-1! Quick!" a witness yelled as he ran for someone to get help.

Eve yelled again, "Sir, I hear you! What's wrong? I hear you! I can't move my legs! I can't move my arms! What's going on?"

Chaos ensued as the sound of ambulance, police sirens, and voices filled the area. There was much clinging and clanging going on around Eve as she called out for help.

"Ma'am, wake up ma'am! Can you hear me? She's not responding!" said the first responder EMT. "She's banged up pretty bad. Let's get her on the gurney so we can get her to the ER STAT!"

"Her pulse is slowly dropping and her heart beat is racing. Ma'am can you hear me? Let me know you can hear me." said the second EMT waiting on Eve's response.

"She's still not responding. Let's get her on an IV so we can see what's going on. She's still alive but she's not responding."

As the EMTs place Eve into the ambulance, a first response officer asked questions of the witnesses in the area. "Sir, I understand you were here when the accident happened, can you give me a report about what you saw?" said the officer.

"Yes sir. I saw the lady's car speeding through the red stop light almost as if someone was chasing her. She wasn't swerving or anything but she just went straight through the light extremely fast. As she entered the intersection, a huge 18 wheeler truck crashed into the side of her car causing her car to flip and spin violently out of control. She landed in the bushes over here on the side of the road and that was when I rushed to park my car and ran over to see if she needed help. She wasn't responding to me when I asked if she was okay so I asked another person who stopped if they could call 9-1-1. That's basically what happened." said the witness as he wrote down his contact information for the officer.

"Okay, Thank you sir. Now, let me go get some other eyewitness reports. We'll keep your information in case we need to contact you for further investigation. You have a nice day."

"Thank you officer, you too." said the witness.

After receiving a disturbing phone call about the accident from one of the officers, James waited patiently in the hospital's emergency waiting area, silently praying and crying. He prayed like he had never prayed a day in his life. He just wished his wife was able to pray with him because he felt when they prayed together their prayers were stronger and reached God directly. He sat down and stood up. He paced the floor in wonder of what could be going on in the back. He sat down and waited patiently for the girls to arrive. He became more impatient as time moved along and no one had yet arrived. He started to feel a little dizzy and weak and wanted someone to be there with him.

The nurse entered the waiting room and explained a little of the incident to James but she made it clear that he would have to wait until the police report was available. As she walked out of the waiting area, the doctor entered, "Hello, I'm Dr. Thomas. Are you Mr. Jacobs?"

"Yes sir I am. What's happening with my wife? How is she? James asked in a panic.

"Mrs. Jacobs is currently in critical condition and we've put her in an induced coma until we can locate where and why she is bleeding. She was bruised up pretty badly but we're working hard to get her back healthy again. There's not a definite time as to when she will wake up but I will send a nurse in to let you know when you can come in to see her. Do you have any questions for me?" asked Dr. Thomas.

"No sir, thanks for the update. Just please let me know something soon." James pleaded.

"Yes sir, we will. If there is anything you need, just let one of the nurses know and they will help you."

James nodded with tears in his eyes, "Thank you."

As he turned around, he heard Janae's voice.

"Daddy what's going on, is mom okay?"

Janae and Lauren finally arrived and James felt a sense of peace with his baby girls there. Lauren was standing behind Janae crying anticipating the worse.

"Well girls, your mom is in a coma. All I know is that she got into it with some woman in the grocery store and when she rushed out, she ran a red light and crashed. I don't know any other details as of yet." James explained.

Lauren felt like her world was crashing down from all that's been going on. Her family had no idea that she was two seconds away from being killed a few nights ago and now this is happening to her mom. She wanted to cry her eyes out for everything else and just spill the beans by letting everyone know what was going on with her but she didn't want to make anything about her so she kept quiet and kept the focus on her mother's health.

"Girls, do you mind if we say a prayer together for y'all mom?" James asked.

The girls nodded their heads and they all joined hands.

"Heavenly Father, I ask of you today to protect and secure my wife's life. Even if she never comes out this coma, please secure her spot in heaven. Please bring my family closer together again and help us to realize that we need each other. Dispatch your angels to be with both of my children and my wife as she lay here on this bed. Amen."

When Janae looked over at Lauren as they said amen, she saw that she was genuinely receiving the prayer. Janae felt so proud of her sister. James could have gone on and on but Dr. Thomas walked in as they were finishing the prayer. He hoped he was coming to bring good news so he made the prayer brief.

"Hello everyone." Dr. Thomas said.

They looked anxiously at him waiting to hear what he had to say.

"We were able to stop Mrs. Jacobs bleeding and we have all of her vitals in stable condition. We discovered that she broke her hip and right arm in the accident. Thankfully, none of her organs were damaged; however, she will require surgery for her hip. After surgery, we should be able to get her back to normal. She is still in the coma and we will keep her in the coma until tomorrow so that we can monitor her. We've placed her in a room and you can come and sit with her. Oh, and even though she's in the coma, she can still hear you as you talk to her." Dr. Thomas said affirming the family that Eve would be okay.

"Thank you Dr. Thomas. When can we see her? asked Janae.

"The nurse will be in shortly to give you her room number so that you may go in to see her.

"Thanks again doctor." said James feeling somewhat relieved.

As Dr. Thomas walked back out of the waiting area, the nurse walked in.

"Mr. Jacobs, Mrs. Jacobs is in room CCU 414. You and your beautiful daughters are more than welcomed to go visit her now. I'll show you to the elevator." The nurse said as she directed them to the nearest elevator.

"When you get upstairs, the Critical Care nurse will buzz the door open for you. They are expecting you.

"Okay thanks" James said politely.

As they entered Eve's room, they all looked at her and started to cry. Lauren walked over to her mother and said "Ma, I can't believe this happened to you. What am I going to do if I lose you? I know we weren't on good terms because I wanted to do my own thing but I never wanted anything like this to happen to you. Mommy you're everything to me and I was hoping that my child would be everything to you."

Lauren didn't realize what she had just said in front of her father and she didn't notice how quick her father looked over at her. Janae smiled for the first time since being here.

"Lauren, are you telling us you're pregnant?" James asked.

"Yes daddy. I am 4 months pregnant." Lauren said bashfully.

James cracked a smile and walked over to his baby girl to show his love. Lauren felt a sense of relief about everyone finding out. She was so tired of hiding it and feeling alone during her pregnancy. Her sister and father both hugged and kissed her. They were filled with joy for this blessing they were about to receive but still, they were still sad that Eve was in a coma and couldn't enjoy the news. James decided to spend the night with Eve so that he could be by her side when she woke up. They stayed for hours reminiscing about the happy times they had when they were little girls and talked about what they were going to do now that James and Eve were going to be grandparents.

As it started getting late, James told the girls to go ahead and go home. He let them know he would be okay and that he would get something to eat from the cafeteria downstairs. He gave his girls kisses so they could go and rest up.

The next morning, Lauren woke up to the best smelling breakfast she had smelled in a long time. She and Money were on steady terms with each other and to be honest, she was shocked. It seems as though the news about their baby made him realize that he did want to be with her after all. He didn't care what kind of grudge his dad had against her family. He still didn't understand what it was about but it didn't matter at this point. He was going to have to accept her family because they have a little one on the way and he wanted his father in his child's life.

Lauren and Money have been staying in an upscale suite as they waited to have their house remodeled. Lauren didn't know that Money was making plans and had more money stashed away with another one of his boys who he grew up with and trusted. Money hoped nothing happened with Malcolm because lately it seemed like all his boy's loyalty was flying out the window and they were dropping like flies in a hot car with the windows closed. Malcolm had over a hundred thousand dollars stashed away for Money for two years and Lauren couldn't be more thankful for it since she wasn't hustling anymore. She wasn't bringing in any money and she needed to worry about her unborn child now.

Money found every chance he could to kiss on Lauren's stomach. He constantly asked her how she was feeling and how the baby was doing. She loved the attention because it reminded her of who she fell in love with in the beginning. As she watched Money talk non-stop about the baby, it made her more and more excited to be carrying his child and she found herself thanking God more than usual.

She had an appointment later that afternoon to find out the sex of the baby and her man was so ready and anxious that he woke up extra early to make sure she ate. They got dressed and headed to the women's care center downtown. As they arrived, her stomach did twirls. Lauren was excited and nervous again as if it was her first visit. She was happy that she had the support that she had been wanting from Money. She was glad he was able to attend one of her appointments. The nurse greeted the two and led them back to their room to get prepared for her check-up.

"You ready baby?" Money asked Lauren as she undressed and sat up on the bed, waiting for Dr. Wilson.

"Yes, but I'm so nervous to know what it is. I want a boy so he can be a junior but I always want a girl that can be my mini me." Lauren said with excitement.

"I honestly don't care what the baby is. I just want a healthy baby." Money said smiling at Lauren.

Lauren smiled back with teary eyes as she recognized the transformation in her man. She knew the news about the baby was softening him up and him feeling regret about how he treated her in their relationship but she was determined to put everything in the past. She didn't want to remember anything of that time so that she could move forward and make the best of their future.

Dr. Wilson stepped into the room interrupting their conversation.

"Hello Ms. Jacobs. How are you today?

"I'm doing good Dr. Wilson." Lauren replied all smiles.

"I see someone is feeling a lot better from the last few visits we had. Have you been taking your prenatal vitamins and eating healthy?" asked Dr. Wilson.

Lauren thought for a moment and wondered had she honestly been doing so. She could've punched herself for the things she'd been putting her baby through with this pregnancy. She was doing more damage than good by stressing over Money and Samantha, fighting with Starr and not to mention hustling and running from Chico. She had gone through a lot in these past few months. More than she should have.

"Yes I've been taking my vitamins but I haven't been drinking water like I should." Lauren said hesitantly.

Dr. Wilson sighed, "Okay Lauren. You need to up your water and make sure you're eating healthy throughout the rest of this pregnancy. It's vital for your baby's health. Do we have a deal?

"Yes ma'am. I know and I'll do better." Lauren promised.

Dr. Wilson grabbed her gel so she could begin the process. As soon as she turned on the computer, they immediately saw their little one. Money moved in closer and grabbed Lauren's hand. Both excited, she felt like a little kid again with the flutters in her stomach. Dr. Wilson smiled at the bond she saw between Lauren and Travis.

"Alright you guys, here are the fingers" Dr. Wilson said. "And if you look right here, here's the spine"

"Wow that's amazing how it looks on the screen!" Lauren exclaimed.

"Yes Ms. Jacobs. It is amazing and from the looks of it, it appears that you both will have a beautiful baby girl."

Lauren and Money both had smiles from ear to ear. They were so excited and Lauren couldn't wait to go shopping for her new baby girl. Everything was good with the baby but Lauren continued to watch her as she fell in love all over again.

"Thank you Dr. Wilson, I appreciate everything." Lauren said as she got up and fixed her clothes.

"No problem honey. Just make sure you aren't stressing and that you get plenty of rest. You can really hinder your child's well-being if you're not careful,"

Lauren was going to make sure that she did everything right going forward but she still couldn't stop thinking about her mother and her health.

As they walked out of the clinic, holding hands and smiling, Lauren asked Money "Baby are you happy?"

"Yeah man, now we need to go shopping for our baby girl. What you want to name her Babe?" Money asked as he opened the door to the passenger side for Lauren to get in.

Lauren sat for a few seconds looking up to the sky with a smile, "Nevaeh Harmony Williams."

Chapter 10

Lauren woke up from her nap with kisses on her neck, the same way Money used to wake her up when they first started dating. When she realized what was going on, she noticed a baby blue bag sitting in front of her that read "Tiffany & Co". She jumped up, grabbed the bag and pulled out a box that had a necklace with a matching bracelet in it. She turned to Money with his chest poked out and his big Kool-Aid man smile and hugged him so tight.

"I love it babe!" Lauren said.

She felt like her love life was getting back to normal. Since she and Money's have been back together, he hadn't laid a hand on her. Money had already taken his shower and he was ready to hit a few stores before they closed.

Lauren was sleeping much more because of the baby and also to keep her mother's situation off her mind as much as could. She tried hard not to stress about it because she wanted to watch out for the baby. She could tell Money was trying to do the same thing for her by giving her 100% of his support

"Alright babe, go grab your jacket, and let's slide." Money said.

"Okay baby, where are we going though? I'm still a little tired."

"I want to grab the baby a few things and then go have dinner" Money said as he grabbed his keys.

Lauren ran to get her jacket and to use the restroom before heading out. Their first stop was the mall. He wanted to go to Foot Locker to get her some shoes. When they got in the store, Money saw some pink and silver infant Jordan's that he wanted to get for her.

"Babe you like these" Money asked.

"Yes I love them, I'm going to grab these all black ones too" Lauren replied. They brought at least 6 pairs of shoes and matching outfits from Foot Locker and then made their way into the Carter's baby store. Money brought up half of the store and Lauren loved every moment. They bought clothes, shoes, and headbands and went to the Babies 'R' Us to get furniture and breastfeeding supplies.

Before they left the mall for the night they walked over to the steakhouse that was attached on the side of the mall. They were able to get a seat as soon as they walked in. The hostess sat them down in a nice cozy booth off in the corner of the restaurant.

"Your waiter will be right with you." The hostess said as she placed the menus on the table and walked away.

"Thank you." Lauren replied

"Good evening, my name is Robert and I'll be your server for tonight. What can I get you started with to drink?" asked the waiter.

"I would like to have a watermelon margarita. Umm, make that a virgin, please." Lauren said.

"I want some patron, no Salt on the edge of the glass though." Money said.

"Would you like to start off with any appetizers?

"No thank you." said Lauren.

"Okay, I'll be right back with your drinks."

When the waiter left, Money looking at Lauren

"You're so beautiful." He said as he stared into her eyes.

Lauren stared back at him and she believed him.

"Money what's making you change? It's like you've been a totally different man." she asked out of curiosity.

"Because the time I was ducking out at my parents, I had time to think. I had a change of heart. I needed to see who was really for me. I didn't know who to trust especially since my right hand man turned on me. I didn't mean to leave you by yourself or to make you feel rejected but I had to do what I had to do at that moment. I want us to get past that Samantha situation. God bless the dead but she didn't mean nothing to me." Money explained.

Lauren felt he was being real about Samantha but she also felt there were more hoes than her.

"Okay but why you felt you needed to put your hands on me? If you say I'm for you and you love me, why did you hit me?" Lauren asked sternly.

"I don't really want to talk about that." Money replied as the waiter returned with their drinks.

"Here you are, virgin watermelon martini for you and a patron with no salt for you. Are you guys ready to order?"

"Yes. I'll have the blue cheese bacon steak with steamed broccoli and a sweet baked potato." Lauren replied.

"And I'll have the garlic butter steak with mixed vegetables and mashed potatoes" said Money.

"Okay, we'll have this out for you in a little. Just let me know if you need anything else and I'll be around to check on you in a little bit." the waiter said as he left to put in their orders.

When the waiter left, Lauren noticed a woman sitting with her friend staring at her and Money. She looked away and waited to look back over there to see if she was just imagining things. When Lauren looked at them again, she saw they were still staring at them.

"Babe do you know them?" Lauren asked Money, pointing at the females.

"Man nah" Money replied not wanting to look in their direction.

Lauren kept her eyes on them and got up to go to the restroom. When she came out of the stall, the female who was staring the hardest at her and Money was waiting for her.

"Your name is Lauren right and the nigga you sitting with is Money, huh?"

Lauren said with an attitude "Depends, who's asking?"

"Trick I'll cut your behind up in here and just so you know my sister is pregnant by your nigga." she said as she pulled out a knife.

Lauren backed up realizing she couldn't get to her pistol because she left her purse at the booth with Money. The female swung the knife at Lauren and Money busted in the bathroom pointing his gun at the woman. She put her hand down and backed up with the knife.

"Hoe take another step and I'll blow your brains out. We can invite your sister in this bathroom to get it too." Money said.

The female walked out of the bathroom quickly to grab her sister and they left. Lauren looked at Money ready to slap him.

"Hurry up Lauren let's go. They probably got me on camera." He said.

Lauren and Money ran out of the restaurant to the car and drove off.

"Travis Williams who was that and who did you get pregnant?"

"Nobody, them groupies lying." Money said.

"Uh no, I don't believe you, you nasty, how you got somebody pregnant and you with me? Nigga you cheated on me

AGAIN?" Lauren screamed. She had all kinds of emotions boiling over and didn't know what to do with it all.

When they got to the hotel, Lauren was still heated. The played it off as they walked through the lobby and into the elevator. They didn't want to cause a disturbance with the hotel but she let lose when they got into their room.

"Babe man you better chill out. I told you I don't know them hos."

Money wasn't looking for things to go down the way they did at the restaurant. He never wanted Lauren to find out about this chick like this and now she and her meddling behind sister had to go and mess things up for him and Lauren.

"Yeah, I smashed her sister but I know I didn't get her pregnant." He thought to himself. "It's probably not my baby anyway. That ho smashed anything that moved so I know I'm not the father."

Money wanted a baby with Lauren and that was it. He didn't want any other children if they weren't with her. Lauren's phone rang.

"Hello?" answering the phone aggravated.

"Lauren are you okay?" James asked hearing the heated argument between Money and Lauren.

"Yes daddy, it's nothing. Just a little disagreement we're having but everything's okay. What's up?" Lauren replied.

"Okay well I was just calling to check up on you, I've been at the hospital and only left to take a shower and to grab more clothes. Janae's been home and she's been attending church so everyone could continue praying for your mother. Were you going to come back up here one of these days?"

"Of course daddy, I've been trying to stay stress-free and take care of my health for the baby. I can't see mommy like that and my blood pressure been high lately." Lauren said rolling her eyes at Money.

He was pouring him a drink and texting while she talked to her dad. He hoped she would just forget about them girls and their whole argument before she hung up. He didn't feel like dealing with this right now.

"Alright well if you need anything just call me, Lauren." James said.

"Ok daddy. I love you." Lauren said as she hung up the phone. She wanted to slap Money in his face, but instead, she went into the kitchen to take her vitamins. She wanted to watch a movie and chill. After about an hour into the movie, Money fell asleep leaving her up by herself. She went to use the bathroom and heard a small knock at the door. She thought it was the maid but it was too late for her to come around cleaning the rooms. She was normally there early in the morning and out of their way before noon.

"Who is it?" Lauren asked in aggravation.

"It's James"

Lauren opened the door to greet her father and noticed a bag from a local Christian store in his hand.

"Hey daddy. You didn't have to stop by. Come on in." Lauren insisted.

"I just wanted to bring you a little something." James said handing Lauren the bag.

"Okay, thanks daddy." As she looked in the bag, she pulled out a beautiful engraved bible with Lauren's name on it. James felt she needed one at all times and he had it engraved as a surprise for her. It wasn't a typical gift that she would ask for but she still was grateful he stopped by and brought one for her since she was feeling down. James sensed that his daughter was in trouble mentally and he wanted to check on her.

"Are you good?" James asked as she placed the bible on her table.

"Yes I'm fine daddy, just got a lot on my mind like I said earlier"

"Okay, where's Money?" he asked.

Lauren rolled her eyes, "He's in the room sleeping."

The entire time James sat in that hotel, he had feelings that he couldn't describe.

"Lauren, why won't you just move back home with us for a while and that way we could help you with your health, the pregnancy, and the baby." James suggested.

"And what am I going to do about Money daddy?"

James sighed and wondered why she was even into him knowing everything he had done to her. He knew Money wasn't right and he always wondered how he could have such a strong hold on his daughter. He knew that all he could do was pray about it and put it in God's hands.

Before James could respond there was a knock on the door. The knock so loud it startled both of them and she almost dropped the glasses of water that she had made for her and her dad.

"Who is it" Lauren asked nervously.

No one responded so Lauren looked out the peep hole to see Money's dad standing there. Money's father never came to their home and she was confused as to why he was at their hotel room. She opened the door while her father sat at the kitchen table with his back turned. "Where's Travis? I keep calling his phone but he isn't answering." Jerry asked.

James recognized that voice and immediately turned around to see if who he was hearing was actually his mind playing tricks on him. He almost fainted when he saw the face of the man who he never wanted to face again.

Chapter 11

James thought he had seen a ghost when standing in front of him was the face of Jerry Williams, his ex-lover from years ago. Jerry was his first and last male relationship. Lauren's father was a bisexual many years ago until he got with Lauren's mother. He was initially using her as a rebound to get over his heartbreak from Jerry. They were like best friends but James always knew in his heart that being with another man was not right. No one knew he was a bisexual or that he was dating Jerry because they kept it on the hush. He was scared of the criticism he would receive from their friends and from his family, because they were Christians.

James also never told Eve or the kids. It was his little secret and he buried it so far in the closet that he was planning for no one to find out. James and Jerry both ran the streets and went to the juke joints with mutual friends but neither of them knew he and Jerry were a couple. James was cool about him and Jerry's relationship and with the fact that no one knew until a rumor that Jerry was messing around with another man spread around the city and got back to him. He was furious with Jerry because he figured out that the other man wasn't him. James had fallen in love with Jerry and when he found out Jerry had cheated on him with another man, his heart was broken.

James met Eve and started dating her to make Jerry jealous but after a couple of months of dating, James began falling in love with Eve. They turned their lives back to God and because they wanted to do what was right, he left the bisexual lifestyle alone. Jerry made sure to never tell Money or his mother that he was once into men either.

"What is he doing here?" James asked in confusion and nervously waiting to see what was about to go down. He felt like the devil was about to rise out of him.

"Nigga I've been looking for you for a while now." Jerry said as he gave James a malicious grin.

Lauren stood in the middle of the floor, staring at them both, wondering how they knew each other since that she's never introduced the families before.

"How do you guys know each other?" Lauren asked.

James still confused and Jerry still with an evil grin on his face, no one answered. Lauren didn't feel right. She felt something was wrong and the animosity in the room was so thick she could cut it with a steak knife. She instantly became nauseous. Hearing the male voices woke Money up from his nap and once he came to, he walked into the living room to see what was happening. Money wondered why James and Lauren were looking at each other the way they were and why his dad was standing in their hotel room.

"Alright. could someone please explain to me what's going on because standing here without anyone talking isn't helping?" Lauren asked.

"What's up y'all? What's going on Pops?" Money asked as he scanned the room.

Jerry never took his attention off his ex-lover. He just stood and stared at him.

"Lauren, baby, listen..." James started to speak feeling guilty and knowing that Jerry was about to air their dirty laundry.

"Don't listen baby that little trick, go ahead and get to the point." Jerry said as he pulled out his gun.

"Yo Dad! What's wrong with you man? Don't be pulling out no straps. This is Lauren's dad and don't call Lauren no trick either. Do you know him?" Money asked walking towards Jerry.

"Yeah I know him very well." Jerry said grabbing his crotch. Money knew something was off and with the gesture his dad just gave, things seemed suspect.

Lauren nervous and afraid ran to the kitchen sink and threw up everything that was sitting on her stomach.

"Baby you good?" Money asked Lauren as he ran to go check on her.

When Jerry saw Money run to Lauren's aide he grew heated. James took a step to check on Lauren and Jerry pointed the gun his way.

"Whoooaaaaa!" everyone panicked.

"Tell them how we know each other, James, because I've been waiting on this day for a very long time." Jerry growled.

Lauren began to cry as she saw the gun pointed at her father. She was confused about this whole situation.

"You left me alone for another hoe and then had the audacity to have this little itty bitty trick with her." Jerry screamed.

"Daddy, what is he talking about?" Lauren cried harder as she ran to her dad's side. She could care less that Jerry had the gun pointed at them. James remained quiet.

"Pops chill on calling her that and put the gun down!" Money yelled.

"Oh, so now you love this girl?" Jerry asked.

"Man she's pregnant with my little girl."

"Oh really, so now you want to save her? I told you beforehand that I had beef with them."

"I didn't think it was some major beef that we couldn't squash so we could get the family together"

"What's going on Travis? Do you know something?" Lauren turned to get Money's attention.

Money ignored Lauren, keeping his attention on his dad.

James blurted out "We dated."

The whole room became silent.

"What Daddy, you gay?" Money yelled with embarrassment.

"Shut up nigga!" Jerry screamed at Money.

Money in his anger punched the wall.

"Yeah WE'RE gay and he had your little girlfriend with the hoe that he was trying to make me jealous with when we broke up. You didn't even love that hoe!" Jerry grinned at James.

"Don't talk about my mother, Jerry!" Lauren said looking back and forth at her dad and Jerry.

"Now I don't know what kind of freaky relationship y'all had going on but y'all need to get that mess together. Pops put the gun down!" Money told Jerry.

"Jerry put the gun down please. You need to turn your life over to God like we did. You knew what we had going on wasn't right and I opened my eyes to that fact after I found out you cheated on me. I fell in love with my wife and God pulled me out of all of that." James said.

Jerry got even madder that James was talking about Eve and God pulled him from the situation when he loved him.

"I didn't cheat on you and that hoe you call a wife ain't a blessing, neither are these little tricks you claim as your kids." Jerry said.

Money quickly ran towards his father and started wrestling with him to get the gun. (POW)

Lauren screamed! James ducked.

Jerry jumped up startled and staring at his son lying on the floor almost lifeless. There was blood running everywhere. Lauren jumped up and ran to hold Money.

Lauren holding Money in her arms screaming and crying hysterically, "Call 9-1-1! Please call 9-1-1! How could you do this? This is your son! My God! Please Travis, don't leave me! Don't leave us! Please Travis! Noooo!"

Jerry shocked the gun went off, threw the gun down to check on Money. "Get up son! Get up son! I didn't mean to shoot you. Get up son!" Jerry screamed.

Instantly, they heard a loud bang at the door and after kicking the door in, the cops burst through.

"Police! Police!" said one officer.

"Get your hands up NOW!" said the other officer.

The neighbors standing in the hall had called 9-1-1 because they heard arguing and loud noises.

Jerry slowly lifting his hands cried, "Okay sir!'

"Put your hands behind your back, sir. You have the right to remain silent...", reciting Jerry his Miranda rights, one of the officers immediately grabbed and handcuffed him.

Two other police came running through the door and grabbed Lauren to keep her from Money's body. As she stood there, she tuned everything out around her. She felt in her heart that Money would wake up. She couldn't believe he had gotten shot. She needed him right now, so there's no way he could die. Lauren began kicking and screaming as the police officers escorted her and James out of the hotel and into the police car for questioning.

James was thankful he and his daughter were safe and made it out alive and even though James didn't like Travis much, he was sad to see him get shot. He knew Jesus was covering them. As James and Lauren stood outside to write their reports and to tell the police what had happened, Lauren couldn't think straight. All she wanted to know was if Money was alive or if he would be okay. Her mind was in a huge fog.

When the EMTs finally brought Money's body down on a stretcher to put him in the back of the ambulance, she ran towards them and attempted to get into the truck.

"Please let me go. I want to go with him." Lauren yelled at the EMT as she rushed the back door of the ambulance.

James ran behind her "Come on sweetheart, calm down. Just wait a minute."

The paramedic told Lauren that she could not ride with them but she could follow them so James and Lauren immediately got into their cars and sped behind the ambulance to the hospital.

Once they arrived at the hospital, Lauren and James were told to sit in the waiting room. Lauren cried uncontrollably and James couldn't stop praying, as he tried to console her. He kept thanking God for the protection of him and Lauren and for Money's healing. James felt so bad for Lauren and didn't want her to stress to the point of going into labor.

"Drink this water Lauren" James said handing Lauren the bottle.

Pushing the bottle of water away, Lauren continued crying.

"Calm down Lauren, for the sake of the baby"

"I can't Dad, it's not as easy as it sounds" Lauren snapped.

James knew she was mad and hurt because she never disrespected him. He left Lauren alone and waited for the doctor to tell them that they could come in and see Money. Five minutes later, Lauren fell to the ground, crying and cursing hysterically because Travis was pronounced dead.

It's been a week since Travis had been killed and Lauren couldn't eat or drink and could barely sleep. She knew it was bad on her body but every time she tried she just couldn't. Staying at her parent's place was the last thing she wanted to do but she appreciated the support she received from Janae and her father. As soon as they left the hospital, James made Lauren grab her belongings from the hotel when the crime scene investigators allowed her to come back home.

When she walked into her room, it was still clean and decorated the way she left it years ago. Janae made sure everything was in order so she could feel comfortable again.

"How are you doing Lauren?" Janae asked as they sat at the table to eat cereal.

"I'm alright for now" Lauren replied solemnly.

Lauren felt lost and confused. She was pregnant and Money was actually more excited than she was about the baby. Her relationship was going great with him and now he's dead. Her mother is still in the hospital fighting for her life. She didn't know what to do. She wanted to talk with Starr but she hasn't spoken to her since the Chico situation. Her body has been feeling a little off and she knows it's because she hasn't been keeping up with herself. She had no appetite and stopped taking her vitamins again.

"Lauren, why don't you come to church with daddy and me this Sunday?" Janae asked hesitantly.

Lauren didn't want to hear anything about going anywhere. She just wanted the sleep that she had been having problems getting for the past week. "No I'm okay" Lauren said as she began to get up from the table.

"Sis all I've been trying to do is support you, which you know I have. I care about your health and the baby's health and just because Money passed, doesn't mean you should give up on her. If anything you need to be stronger for y'all child. You're going about things the wrong way. I'm trying not to be hard on you but I'm really about to release the beast"

Lauren snickered a little at Janae's comment because she knew her sister was strong but she never heard her say she'll release the beast. She didn't know she had it in her. Seeing Lauren smile made Janae's day because it was her first time smiling since Money had passed.

"See, look at that beautiful smile. Man, Lauren please eat something. I'll cook whatever you have a taste for" Janae said.

Lauren thought long and hard just to test her sister and to see if she was serious. "Okay, I want a steak with onions and bell peppers, a side of mash, corn and dirty rice" Lauren said playfully feeling as though Janae wasn't serious.

"Okay I'll run out and grab the steak and corn because we don't have any. Give me a little while and I got you. You better eat it though because this is a full course meal." Janae said smiling.

"Okay I will" Lauren smiled back.

"Before I leave, do you mind if I read you a bible verse?" asked Janae.

"Go ahead Janae, that's what you're good for other than being my sister"

Janae just needed her sister to hear the word of God because she knew within her heart of hearts that one day Lauren would realize what's going on and that she would take heed to everything she's being told. "Lauren God's got you. He's got you more than you'll ever know. You just keep ignoring him and he is trying to get your attention. He will be everything you need if you stop pushing him to the side."

"Okay, Janae, could you come on with the verse because your preaching is starting to sound like mommy" said Lauren.

Janae pulled out her bible and found a verse for her to hear. "Jesus asked do you finally believe? But the time is coming, indeed it's here now, when you will be scattered, each one going its own way, leaving me alone. Yet I am not alone because the father is with me. I have told you all this so that you may have peace in me. Here on earth you will have many trails and sorrows, but take heart because I have overcome the world."

Janae finished reading and felt a sense of peace hoping Lauren felt the same. Lauren just sat staring at the wall. Janae could tell she was in deep thought so she grabbed her car keys and told her she would be back then left to get her food.

Lauren was finally able to take a two-hour nap and she woke up and scheduled a doctor's appointment for the next day. Her feet were beginning to swell badly and her vision started getting blurry. The next day, Lauren arrived at the clinic. They went through the usual of checking her in and setting her in the back room to wait for the doctor.

After checking her blood pressure, Dr. Wilson said it was high. Lauren began to stress even more considering all the things she had been going through and now concerned for her unborn child.

"Lauren are you stressing a lot?" Dr. Wilson asked.

Lauren nodding her head no just sat in silence.

"Ms. Jacobs is there anything you need to speak with me about? I need to know about your health and well-being so that I can make sure the baby is fine."

"No, I'm okay. It has been a lot going on but I'm okay" Lauren replied turning her head away.

Dr. Wilson knew there was something wrong with Lauren and that there was more to the story. She needed to at least know if Lauren would be okay even if she didn't want to speak with her about it.

"Honey, I'm going to need you to work on taking care of yourself if you want any hope for your little one. You're on your way to developing preeclampsia and we don't want that for you" Dr. Wilson explained.

Lauren knew she hadn't been taking good care of herself but she didn't want anything major to happen to her or her baby. She was trying to stay strong for her and her daughter but she felt like her whole world was crumbling. Dr. Wilson let Lauren listen to her daughter's heartbeat and that seemed to be the only thing to calm down Lauren's mind for the moment. Her heart was going strong and Lauren felt she couldn't continue to not take care of herself no matter the situation. Dr. Wilson finished checking Lauren out and prescribed her a very low dose of blood pressure medicine to help maintain her pressure until her next appointment.

She sat in her car thinking about her life and feeling she truly needed a change because her heart couldn't handle the death and disloyalty that was coming her way. When she arrived back at her parent's house, she was preparing to take a shower and crawl into bed when she ran into her father in the hall.

"Whoa Dad, what are you doing here? I thought you were at work!" Lauren asked fearfully.

"Oh, I didn't mean to scare you. I'm on a two hour lunch break today and decided to come home and check on you and Janae. I called your sister because she isn't here and she told me she was out running errands" James replied.

James and Lauren hadn't talked about his homosexual past, since finding out about it at the hotel. They've only spoken about the death of Money and what Lauren's next step would be going forward. Lauren knew the subject needed to be touched on sooner or later because it was the pink elephant in the room now that the commotion with Money was over.

"Daddy, we have to talk and we can't dance around the topic" Lauren said.

"Yeah I knew we would. I just needed time to think about everything a little more. I needed to figure out how I wanted to fill you all in." James replied with his head down.

They both sat silently in the living room trying to gather their thoughts and the words to say to each other. Breaking the silence, Lauren asked, "What made you attracted to men and did you ever step out on mommy with a man?"

"I've never stepped out on your mother. I promise it was JUST us and no one else. The relationship with Jerry was before your mother and nothing made me gay. I was in college and I was curious. I was in the streets and found someone I was attracted to.

We started talking as friends and then began dating. No one knew about our relationship because it could've messed up my reputation." James replied.

He started to feel nervous talking to Lauren about his past and he didn't want her to judge him even though he wasn't into men.

"Did mom know you were bisexual?"

"No she didn't. I met your mother after we had broken up. She knew that I was heartbroken over someone but she thought it was another woman. She was being a friend and helping me through that whole ordeal. During that time, I ended up falling in love with your mother, so that's why Jerry said that I had left him for a woman."

Lauren didn't take her father to be that type of man. He was so manly, muscular, and strong. She couldn't imagine him in bed with another man or even having feelings for another man.

"Your mother and I got real serious and we both found God. I needed him because I was confused and I knew that I was going down the wrong path. I knew that I was supposed to be with a woman but I needed God to help me to get rid of the feelings that I had for Jerry. Your mother helped me on the better path to seeking God whether she knew it or not. I needed your mother then and I definitely need her now. We have to stay strong for her and believe that she'll make it through" James replied as he comforted Lauren.

Lauren couldn't stop thinking about her mom and she wanted to be with her because she needed her. She needed her more than anything in the world right now.

"Can we go and see mom tomorrow please? I just need to let her know I'm still here for her." Lauren asked anxiously.

"Yeah definitely, you, Janae, and I will go visit her." James replied.

"I think I'm going to get some rest. I really need to go to sleep" Lauren told James.

James was glad that she was coming to her senses because he knew she wasn't getting any rest but he was determined to continue praying for her.

Chapter 12

When Lauren, her father and Janae reached the hospital they were more than ready to see Eve. She was still in a coma but the family continued to speak to her as if she was able to talk back to them. They had a huge amount of hope that she would be okay. James had some of the pastors from their church and some of their pastor friends come to visit and to pray over her. James never left without saying a prayer for her or reading her a bible verse.

When Lauren entered the room she felt weak. It was as if her soul had left her body for a second but she got herself together and composed herself enough to sit in the chair close to her mother. Janae and James sat a little further away so they could give Lauren room to speak freely with her. Because Lauren hadn't seen Eve in a while, they knew she would break down.

Lauren grabbed Eve's arm and kissed her hand gently. She regretted the calls and texts she'd missed from her mom. She wished she would've answered and texted back to all of them.

"Ma, it's me, Lauren. I miss you so much. I need you to wake up ma. I don't know what I'm doing out here without you. I feel like I'm barely making it and it's getting to me." Lauren spoke softly with tears welling in her eyes.

"I found out what I'm having. It's a girl and I will name her Nevaeh Harmony Jacobs" she said with a slight smile.

Lauren decided to change the baby's last name back to hers since Money was longer with them. She thought it was only right. "Mommy, Money is dead. The story is so long, I don't know where to start but he is gone and I'm now by myself. I've been staying at the house with Janae and daddy. We need you there." Lauren said as she began crying.

Janae walked over to her and softly rubbed her back. Just as Janae started to say something, a white male walked into the room. Everyone looked because he wasn't wearing a doctor's or nurse's uniform. He looked like a wealthy man and was well put together. James immediately stood up and asked, "Hello sir, what room are you looking for?"

The man ignored James and walked over to Eve's bedside. He stood over and looked deeply at her motionless body.

James, Lauren and Janae all looked at each other in confusion and wondered what was going on. Janae walked out of the room and to the nurse's station to ask who this man was. Eve's nurse came into the room to see who the unknown man was.

"Oh, this is Eve's family. This isn't his first time visiting. He's been here before." She said as she left the room. It was as if everything was normal. Once the nurse left, James walked over to the man.

"Excuse me, may I ask how you are related to Eve?

The male stood quietly and looked up into James' eyes. "Thank you." he said.

"What's your name and why are you thanking me?" James asked.

"My name is Marc Christopher and I'm thanking you for many reasons" the man replied.

The room grew silent and everyone looked around at each other while Marc looked back down at Eve. He took his attention off Eve and looked over at Janae with a spark in his eyes.

James immediately said "She's underage. Now who are you?"

"Oh no, I would never look at her in such manner, I'm just looking at her" replied Marc.

Janae began to get nervous. She was confused. "Mr. Christopher, could you have a seat and tell us who you are?" Janae asked nervously.

Lauren carelessly walked over to the window and began looking outside. She wasn't concerned with who this Marc man was because it wasn't going to bring her mother out of the coma so she ignored him. Marc took a seat and continued to stare at Eve.

"Who are you?" James asked as he began to get aggravated with Marc.

"I'm an old friend of Eve's" Marc replied briefly.

"Okay well, the nurse said you were a family member. What kind of friend are you to my wife?" James asked with an attitude to let Marc know that he was getting pissed.

Marc looked around and he finally said, "My name is Marc Christopher and I'm Janae's biological father."

Janae's mouth dropped opened while Lauren turned quickly from staring out of the window. James couldn't believe what he was hearing and he almost snapped. The whole room was shocked and no one knew what to say next.

"What do you mean you're Janae's biological father?" James yelled.

Lauren ran to James' side to calm him down but he moved Lauren to the side so she wouldn't touch him. They've never seen their father like this and didn't know if they ever wanted to again.

"Yes, I am her biological father. Look at her" Marc replied calmly. He was prepared for this type of outrage but didn't know it would erupt now and with Eve lying in a coma. James and Lauren both looked over at Janae and they honestly admitted in their minds that she did resemble this guy but they were confused as to how. How this could happen when the only man Eve had ever been with was their father was beyond words at this moment.

"Please explain" Janae calmly replied to Marc.

"Janae, first, I just want to apologize to you. Your mother and I had an affair. I knew she was married and I was in a serious relationship myself but at the time I wasn't married"

James, angry with what he was hearing, jumped out of his chair and ran up on Marc. As he got to Marc, two nurses burst through the door to see what the chaos was about. Janae screamed at her dad, "No, Dad, sit down! Stop! Not right here and not right now!"

She honestly wanted to hear what this man had to say. James composed himself and walked to the opposite side of the room, angry and ready for anything to pop off. The nurses walked back out of the room once they saw things were calming down. James knew behaving this way was ungodly but he was hurt, confused and ready to snap on anything in sight. He felt betrayed and his old temper started to come back. He stood quietly in the corner taking a moment to pray to God to help him with his self-control.

"Okay Mr. Christopher, continue" Janae said as she sat back down in. Lauren stood in the middle of the room by her mother, just in case something went down, and stared at Mr. Christopher to see how this story was going to play out.

"Eve and I messed around for about a year. I didn't want anyone to know because I had a relationship at home and she agreed because she had her own thing going on. We wanted each other deeply. Your mother was everything to me but I just didn't know what to do anymore so I called it all off. There was no way we could live normal lives while sneaking around with each other." Marc said shaking his head in disappointment.

"When I called to break it off with her, she was calling me to tell me that she was pregnant and that the baby was mine. She told me that she knew it was mine because at the time, her and James weren't having sex at all." he explained.

James knew exactly what Marc was talking about because at the time she conceived Janae, Eve was working two jobs and she was always too tired. They had gone a whole month without having sex. He wanted to respect her because she was tired and he didn't want to push it or force her into something she didn't want to do. In James' mind he thought he was being the husband she needed at that moment but in reality, Eve was having sex with Marc. Because James didn't push the issue, she gave herself to Marc freely.

"When she called to tell me she was pregnant, we both planned to make it appear to be James' baby. She wanted to keep her marriage and I wanted to keep things good between me and my now wife" Marc said.

Janae chimed in "So you basically didn't want me is that what you're saying? And who is your wife now?"

"Yes I wanted you but I felt the situation was too messy back then. I also knew that I would have to face you and James one day. I just didn't know when that day would come. I'm sorry to say this but my wife's name is Justine. She was the one who caused all of this in the first place, so I figured the time was now" Marc said.

"Wait, what did she cause?" Lauren asked as she walked closer to him.

"Before Eve got into the accident, she had a fight with Justine in a grocery store. As Eve was trying to get away from it, the crash happened. Justine knew about Eve and Janae and about the deal Eve and I made to keep it quiet. I told her about everything 2 years ago and she's had a grudge against Eve ever since. She saw her at the store and they started fighting. Now she's being questioned by the police about it. I've been having the feeling that I need to leave her too." he replied.

"No, if you feel you need to come back into my wife's life because you feel guilty for this you could forget about that. She's married and after today you'll never see her again" James said trying hard to keep his composure.

Janae didn't know what to say so she just sat trying to process everything Marc had confessed to. Lauren wanted to kill this man because it was his wife who caused her mother end up in this situation. She felt so bad for Janae having to hear this information in this way so she walked over to her and caressed her hair.

"No don't touch me!" Janae said as she moved Lauren's hand away from her.

Lauren pulled her hand away quickly hoping her sister was okay. Janae felt overwhelmed. All she wanted was for her mother to wake up and to confirm or deny everything Marc has just bombarded her with. Even though she was in shock, she felt deep in her heart that Marc was telling the truth.

As Janae pondered on what was just said, she immediately remembered overhearing her mother on a phone conversation. Eve wouldn't say any names on the phone when she was speaking to her friend that grew up with named Rhonda. James wasn't home so she spoke freely thinking that Janae was still taking a nap. Janae didn't care about the conversation because she didn't think it was about her until she began to have these weird dreams. She then started to see a few signs here and there.

Janae began praying in the room and everyone stared at her. Marc walked closer to hug her until James stopped him.

"Step away from her. Mr. Christopher, I'm the only man she's known as a father and I'm the only one she's going to know as father. I've been here all of her life from watching her birth, seeing her first steps, teaching her first words, sending her off to kindergarten and so forth so you can't just step into her life and expect to take her back home to your family or feel as though she's supposed to run into your arms. I'm still her father" James said firmly.

"Okay, I can respect that. I didn't say I wanted to come and take her back home. I only needed for her to know the truth" said Marc.

"I just want to know why. Why didn't you own up to having an affair with my mom and making me in the process and why couldn't tell your wife about me until now" Janae asked as she began to cry.

"Because your mother and I were both in the wrong and we were young. You're my first daughter but you're her second. I honestly wasn't ready to take care of a child, so when she came up with that suggestion I went along with it. Now I regret it because I do want you in my life. I want to experience things with you that a father should with his first born daughter. Seeing how I am with my second child, I can only sit and imagine how things would've been if I had just stayed and stuck it out with you"

"So I have another sibling?" Janae asked.

Marc smiled and said "Yes, you have a younger brother, his name is Alex."

"Okay I think it's time for us to leave" James said as he grew aggravated by the minute. He couldn't take another minute in that room with this man and prayed Eve would wake up so that they could get everything cleared up. This hurt him badly but he knew he had a few things in his past that he wasn't proud of either. This was his wife and she's in a coma so he had no choice but to stay by her side for better or for worse.

"Dad, we should invite Mr. Christopher and his son to dinner" Lauren suggested.

Janae and James looked at Lauren like she was crazy but a piece of Janae wanted to have dinner with them. James looked at Janae for approval because if it was left up to him, he would've whooped his behind to the point of him never wanting to step foot near any one of them again.

"Daddy, I think I need this" Janae replied shyly.

James walked over to Eve and gave her a kiss on the forehead. He left Lauren and Janae in the room and went to the car.

"Could we exchange numbers Janae?" asked Marc as he handed her his cell phone.

Janae grabbed the phone and put her number in it. While giving him back the phone, she gave him one last look over and at that moment she saw all of her in his eyes. She knew deep down that he was her father. She got up and walked out of the hospital room with her sister.

Chapter 13

Lauren tried to give Janae her space so she could take in everything that happened the other night. James had been quiet due to the news he had heard about Eve. He wanted to stay calm especially with Janae meeting up with Marc. Lauren supported her because she felt Janae needed to know the truth and that she needed to get to know her brother. James would always be their father but it wouldn't hurt to build a cordial relationship with Marc.

Janae had been in her room praying for everyone and was still trying to wrap her brain around the fact that James was not her real father. Lauren missed her sister and felt bad this was happening to her. She wanted to be there for her more than anything because Janae has never turned her back on her when things got rough.

There was a knock on Jane's door.

"Who is it?" Janae asked.

"It's me, Lauren. Are you hungry or thirsty Janae?" she asked.

"I'm thirsty. I would take water if you don't mind"

Lauren ran to get the water from the fridge in hopes of Janae talking to her when she returned. She didn't want to force her to speak about it if she wasn't ready but she definitely wanted to be that shoulder that she could lean on. Lauren returned back to Janae's room with her water and noticed the bible lying on the bed.

"Janae, why do you never question God about how he could let this happen?" Lauren asked.

"Lauren you never question God. You just pray and he reveals answers when the time is right. God doesn't put more on you than you can bear. I'm hurt by what's going on but I can't blame God" Janae said as she looked back down at her bible.

"Okay but how could he let something like this happen with you being so close to him?"

"It was no one but the devil that tempted Mommy and Marc to commit adultery. They gave in to him because it was what they wanted to do. God didn't have anything to do with that. God has kept me and he's never let me hit rock bottom because I pray to him on the daily. I believe in him. He's kept me fed and breathing, so I could never look at him like he was wrong and you shouldn't neither Lauren"

Lauren stopped speaking because she didn't want Janae to turn things on her.

"So how are you feeling?" Lauren asked.

"I'm okay Lauren"

"How do you feel about having dinner with him and your brother, honestly?"

Lauren felt weird even asking that because it's always been just her and Janae or so they thought.

"I'm ready to meet Alex and I need to know more about Marc but I keep wondering if there is anyone else who knows about this" Janae questioned.

Lauren wondered the same thing. "Okay so, do you want to meet him here or at a restaurant?"

"I want to meet at a restaurant just out of respect for daddy you know. I barely know this man so I'm really not ready for him to come to my home" Janae mentioned.

"Okay cool, well I'm definitely going with you. Send him a text telling him to meet you at the Chinese buffet by 33rd" Lauren motioned.

Janae grabbed her phone and sent the text to Marc. She noticed that she had missed a call from an unknown number. She was getting ready to call the number back when the number called in again

"Hello?" Janae answered her phone.

"Janae, this is Starr. Please pray for me." Then the phone hung up. Janae looked at the phone and wondered what had just happened. Why did Starr just call saying to pray for her and then hung up the phone. She thought maybe it was a prank call but the caller didn't block their number. When Janae called the number back, it went directly to voicemail.

"Lauren, that was Starr who just called me. She told me to pray for her and then she hung up"

Lauren sat up on the bed shocked because she hadn't spoken to Starr since she saved her from Chico's hunt to kill her. She was curious about why she wanted Janae to pray for her and she was hoping Starr hadn't gotten herself into anything crazy. Lauren worried about her friend. Even though she didn't mention anything about Samantha and Money at first and she caught her doing drugs in her bathroom, she was still a great friend to her and Lauren loved her.

"When's the last time you spoke to her?" Janae asked.

"Oh my god, it's been a while but I miss her like crazy. I've tried going by her place but it was empty like she had moved. I tried calling her grandmother's number and I couldn't get in contact with anyone" Lauren said.

Janae received a text back from Marc confirming to meet the girls later that night. She was nervous as she read the text but she was going to go through with it. She knew that through the grace of God, he would definitely be by her side and get her through it.

"What are you going to wear Janae?" Lauren asked as she started scanning through Janae's closet. She had nothing but sundresses and floral blouses. She saw Janae didn't have much of a choice.

"Don't look at my closet like that Lauren, that's what I choose to wear and I'm comfortable wearing what I wear. You don't have to dress like a slut to be seen. I am a woman of God and I dress how I want to be approached" Janae said as she got up to fix her hair in her mirror. Janae's words sort of struck a chord with Lauren because she dressed provocative and she didn't have any clothes to cover her up.

James arrived home and quietly peeked in to see the girls talking in Janae's room. He felt somewhat better as he saw Janae crack a smile at Lauren while she checked herself out in the mirror. James walked by Janae's door and stood there. When the girls noticed him there they stopped talking and looked at him.

"Hey girls" he said

Lauren and Janae walked over to him and gave him a big hug together. He felt loved and he didn't want to let them go. It reminded him of when they were little girls and when he got home from work, they would run to the door and jump on him at the same time. James would give anything to get that back but the girls showing that same love at the moment meant everything to him.

"I'm going to meet Marc with Lauren at a restaurant tonight. Do I have your blessing Daddy?" Janae asked her father as she pulled away from him to look into his face.

"Yes Janae you can go. You're grown and you need to know the truth. I can't stop you from doing what you think is right" he responded.

"Thanks Daddy. You don't have to worry. We'll be okay. Lauren is going to go with me so I'm not by myself." Janae said as she and Lauren gave him a kiss on the cheek and went back into her room.

James trusted Janae and felt she would do the right thing. He knew his daughter was mature and strong minded so he wasn't worried about this random guy stringing her along. He felt peace knowing that Lauren was going to tag along and that Janae wouldn't be by herself. He knew without a shadow of doubt that Lauren would snap if anything happened to her sister. He raised his girls to support and stand by each other, they were not just beautiful but they were smart and strong. He was a proud father and he was not about to let anyone take that away from him.

Later that night, as Lauren and Janae arrived at the buffet; they didn't see Marc anywhere in sight. Lauren made reservations earlier after Janae received the confirmation text back from him. The hostess sat them at their table but there was no Marc. Janae texted his phone and waited a while to give him time to respond. Lauren had ordered herself a glass of water and a little plate of lo mien. Janae had no appetite; she was just ready to meet Marc and his son Alex. Her stomach was in knots waiting for them to arrive.

"Umm, so did he text back yet?" Lauren asked curiously.

"No which is weird. It's been twenty minutes already. I'm not trying to blow him up but gosh, he knew the time so he should've been here by now." Janae ordered herself a sweet tea and an egg roll to get something in her stomach as they waited.

Forty minutes into them waiting Janae decided to give Marc a call. The automated system answered saying this phone number was out of service. Janae was confused thinking maybe she had dialed the wrong number so she went to her messages and hit the call button from the text he had sent her previously. The automated system answered again. Marc's phone was off and she was livid.

"What is going on with this dude, man?" Janae blurted out.

Lauren looked trying to figure out what her sister was screaming about. "Lower your voice Janae, what's wrong with you? What's the problem?" she asked.

"I called his number twice and his phone is turned off" Janae replied.

"Do you mean turned off as in its just going to voice-mail or... "

Janae cut her off "No I mean turned off as in the service on the phone is no longer working. I don't have any other contact information for him."

She was furious because she took the time out to come and he couldn't even let her know he genuinely wasn't interested in meeting with her. She felt abandoned again by a man that she just met and he had the audacity to cut his service off and not even contact her with a new number. Lauren started to feel bad for her sister.

"It's okay Janae, please don't let this get to you, let's just wait a little longer" Lauren recommended.

"No, I was good before I met him and I'll be good afterwards. I'll have a long talk with God because I know he always got me" Janae said. They finished their meal to give Marc twenty more minutes to show but he was a no-show.

"Talk to God" Lauren said breaking the silence. Janae face lit up like she'd seen a ghost. She was already going to do that but hearing her sister say it made her feel good. She cracked a smile at Lauren and said "Yeah, maybe you should try it too sis." as they walked out of the restaurant to go home.

The next morning, Lauren laid in her room trying to figure out what to say. She stared at the ceiling just thinking about life. She knew she needed God but she felt she was good figuring things out on her own. "God?" she questioned within herself. God is who she needs to turn to, he is her savior and she needed to realize that. Lauren found it hard to sit and pray, even with everything going on in her life, she still hadn't sought God for help.

She grew up in church but everyone could tell she wasn't spiritually in tune. She thought about her life and how she could change and make the best out of it. She wanted everything to work out for the better especially with her new baby on the way. "I just want better for me and my baby. I just wish I knew how to make it better." She mumbled under her breath. It seemed as if everyone around her and everything in her life was spiraling out of control.

She planned to cook dinner for everyone because she wanted her father to feel as though her mom was still in the house. She wanted to have a well-cooked full course meal waiting for him as he arrived home from work and she wanted her sister to eat since she had a low appetite but needed to run to the store for a few things.

She decided to make chili with garlic knots because that was her father's favorite and ever since they were children Janae never could turn down some buttery garlic knots.

Lauren decided to walk to the convenience store two blocks away since she didn't have her car. The day was a bit gloomy. It was cold and you barely could see through the thick layer fog. There weren't many people out and Lauren was thankful for that because she didn't want to run into someone she knew. She really wasn't in the mood to talk to anyone right now. As Lauren walked down to the first block and crossed over the street, a woman, who looked to be in her mid-forties, sitting at the bus stop, stopped her and asked for a minute of her time.

"Hello Miss, are you doing okay?" the woman asked.

Lauren didn't know who she was and didn't plan on speaking to her but she figured the woman just needed someone to chat with.

"Yes I'm fine." Lauren said as she started to continue on her walk.

The woman looked at her with worry in her eyes and Lauren became concerned.

"God told me to let you know that everything will blow over and that you will be just fine." the woman responded to the look in Lauren's face.

Lauren was curious as to why she stopped her to tell her that. She didn't know whether she should believe her or whether the woman was just another lunatic crack head talking. The woman wasn't dressed the best as she wore dingy jeans and a loose t-shirt with plain white sneakers that were possibly a few years old. Her hair was tied up in a bun. The woman's skin was smooth but Lauren thought maybe she was one of those well-kept crack heads.

Lauren nodded her head at the woman in hopes of ending the conversation and began to walk off hoping she didn't follow. The woman knew Lauren didn't want to discuss the Lord with her so she didn't push it. She delivered the message as he had told her to and she was satisfied that she had done her job and continued waiting for the bus to arrive.

Lauren finally reached the store still thinking about what the woman had shared with her. She grabbed everything she needed and as she was standing at the register getting checked out, she spotted someone that looked familiar to her. The girl was standing on the corner begging for drugs and she looked like life had beaten her down. When Lauren stepped out of the store she took a good look at the girl and realized that it was Starr.

Starr was down on her knees begging a young drug dealer to give her some drugs and she'll pay him back. Knowing full well the dealers around their way didn't work like that, she still tried. Lauren called Starr's name and she turned to look her way. Starr still on her knees looked Lauren's way as the dealer walked away. When Starr realized it was Lauren she slowly got up and attempted to run the other way.

"Starr do not try me like that" Lauren screamed.

Starr stopped dead in her tracks and turned around slowly with her head down. Lauren walked over to her and stared her in her eyes. Starr brushed herself off trying not to look as bad as she did. She wore white jean shorts that had turned gray, a black wife beater with holes in it and mix matched sandals. Her hair was messy and everywhere like it hadn't been combed. Everything she had on looked as though she got it from a dump and Lauren figured she was probably prostituting herself to get drugs too.

"What happened to you Starr?" Lauren asked her friend worried for her.

"What do you care?" Starr shot back at Lauren with attitude.

"What you mean what do I care? Even though we had a fight at your house, it doesn't mean I don't care for you Starr. You're still my friend and you saved me from Chico." Lauren expressed.

"You cut me off like it was nothing. You didn't even call or anything after that day. I should've let him kill you."

Lauren felt a little hurt by her comment but she didn't show it because she knew she was going through.

"You let yourself go Starr. Why are you doing this to yourself?"

"After losing my apartment because I was short on rent, I began using drugs as my outlet and you see it got the best of me" Starr said sarcastically. She smiled and Lauren saw that she was missing a few teeth. She figured that she must have gotten into a street fight with someone or a dealer put their hands on her. The way her teeth were missing, it had to be that a guy had knocked her out.

"Why are you being sarcastic? Can you come back to my parent's house and clean yourself up Starr?"

"Listen Lauren, I'm good. I'm ok with how I'm living, I'm on my last leg anyways and I ain't got time for your extra behind" Starr said as she was about to turn and walk away.

Lauren grabbed her arm. "So you're content with how you're living? You don't have a house or money. You're on drugs and I'm pretty sure you're prostituting. You're a bum and that ain't cute" Lauren said angrily because she had turned her offer down.

"Trick you don't know what I got and what I don't got. Just leave me alone and go back to your good ol' stuck up behind lifestyle"

"You know what I've been going through so why would you say that?"

"Cause trick, your life sure better than mine right now, so you're good"

"Starr, you have a chance to clean yourself up and get back right. Boss status, how you were before all this" Lauren said.

"I wasn't a boss. I was delusional. I was working a lame 9-5 and trying to keep up with the Joneses. My stupid behind had sex with Chico and let him take advantage of me. Good thing I killed that nigga though because even if I did get clean again, I'll forever feel dirty with the AIDS that he gave to me." Starr said tearfully.

Lauren's mouth dropped at what she just heard. She had no clue Starr had hooked up with Chico. No wonder she started acting funny towards him and to hear that he gave her a disease, she felt even worse for her friend. She didn't know what to say anymore. Lauren looked into Starr's eyes and could tell she wanted to break down crying. Starr explained how she lost her apartment and her grandmother within the same week. She knew she couldn't reach out to Lauren since she had learned that she was back with Money on the streets. She knew Lauren had things going on herself.

Starr kept her distance and stayed to herself sleeping on a dirty mattress inside an abandoned crack house. She sold her body for food and money for crack but lately it's been slow. The men that wanted the hoes on the streets weren't looking Starr's way. She was getting washed up to the old men who were looking for a quick trick in the late hours of the night.

Lauren chimed in, "Starr did you call my sister's phone one night asking her to pray for you?"

Starr didn't respond. She looked down at her shirt and picked at it like something was on it to ignore the question.

"I know you hear…"

"Yes" Starr interrupted. "I called her, at that moment, because I was crying from getting half of my teeth knocked out. I didn't want to be in this predicament anymore. I felt if Janae prayed for me, God would hear her before he heard me."

Lauren felt a strong urge to grab Starr and she held her friend. "Everything will be okay and if you pray I guarantee you God will hear you Starr. Don't feel like you're less than anyone because I know you aren't" Lauren comforted her.

"Have you started praying or are you still acting like there isn't a God?" Starr asked.

"I know there's a God, I've just been trying to handle things on my own but I pray from time to time." Lauren lied.

Starr gave her the side eye knowing good and well, Lauren was lying. Lauren needed to get back to the house so she could prepare dinner but didn't want to leave Starr alone without being able to keep in contact with her.

"I'm guessing you don't have a phone?" Lauren asked.

"Yeah but I don't have money to keep minutes on this prepaid crap" Starr replied.

Lauren wrote her number down and begged Starr to call her if she needed anything. "I love you Starr. I know everything will be just fine with you" as she hugged her.

"Love you too Lauren"

Lauren watched Starr as she walked away feeling like she should've done more to stop her from going down that route but Starr is a grown woman and there wasn't much she could do if Starr didn't want to change.

Chapter 14

"Lauren wake up! Wake up!" James screamed as he ran into Janae's room to wake her up. "Wake up Janae! Get up girls!" he yelled.

The girls woke up confused and thought something bad had happened. Lauren shot up out of bed and ran straight for her closet to get her pistol from her duffle bag. James had no clue she had brought the gun into the house but before she ran out her room ready to shoot the first thing that wasn't supposed to be in the house, she heard her father yell from the hallway.

"Put on some clothes. We have to go to the hospital!"

Lauren was glad she didn't get into the hallway with her pistol because she did not want to hear his mouth about having a gun. James had received a call from the hospital asking for him to get there as quickly as possible. James prayed long and hard hoping to see Eve up and out of the coma. It had been a while and though the hospital had put her in a medically induced coma the night the accident happened, when the doctors and nurses took her out of the medical coma, she remained in a natural coma.

Janae and Lauren were half sleep as they rode with their father to the hospital at 3 o'clock in the morning. Janae began saying a prayer in her head and they both hoped to see Eve awake. She praised and worshiped God from excitement and because she believed in the power of prayer. She felt all type of chills through her body but they weren't making it to the hospital fast enough.

"Daddy, everything is good right? Did they tell you if she was awake or not?" Lauren asked concerned about their need to rush to the hospital this early in the morning.

"No they didn't say if she was awake. The nurse called and asked me to come up there as soon as I could. I barely let her finish her sentence before I woke you guys up to come with me" James replied.

James didn't know what to expect either but he would soon find out because he was pulling up into the hospital. As they arrived, he walked to the guest services desk

"Hello, how may help you?" asked the guest services rep.

"Yes, I received a call from the nurse telling me to come up as soon as possible." James replied.

She asked for his information and told him to have a seat in the waiting area.

Ten minutes passed and they were still waiting. The girls were beginning to doze off in their chairs and grew impatient. They just wanted to know if their mother was awake or not. After thirty minutes, James walked back to the receptionist, "Excuse ma'am, can you please find out the nurse that contacted me and have her to contact me? It's almost four thirty in the morning and I need to know what's going on with my wife. They called me to come up here."

"Okay one moment sir" the receptionist said as she could sense the aggravation coming from James. As she picked up the phone to make the call, a doctor came to greet James. The girls were still balled up sleeping on their comfy sofas. Lauren's phone rang and it woke her up. She wondered who was calling her at this time of the day. It was a number not saved in her phone so she quickly answered it.

"Hello" Lauren said.

The caller said nothing but Lauren could hear them breathing. Lauren got scared thinking that maybe it was an enemy. She hoped someone was playing with her. She hung up the phone and called the number back but got no answer. She looked over to see her father speaking with a doctor so she went to join the conversation to find out what was going on with her mother.

"I apologize, Mr. Jacobs" the doctor said as Lauren walked up.

James looked shocked and stunned but he wasn't crying.

"When you're ready, you and your girls can come see her" the doctor said before his pager went off and he stepped to the side to take a call.

"Oh my gosh daddy, is ma awake?" Lauren asked excitedly.

James didn't respond. He took a seat and stared at the floor.

"Dad what's wrong?" Janae asked as she woke up.

Lauren was ready to see her mother. "Daddy, what's wrong? Why aren't you talking?"

After a few minutes, James spoke "Girls, I can't believe it but your mother didn't make it."

Janae fell to the floor crying as Lauren hit the wall. Both of the girls cried hysterically while James tried his best to calm them both down. They all hugged in the middle of the waiting room while people stared at them with empathy. James said a prayer as he hugged the girls. They both became weak at the knees and felt like they were about to drop to the floor.

"Father God, I'll never question you upon why you took Eve. I will miss my wife dearly but my only concern would be if she made it up to you. We know she's in a better place but father I ask you to please keep me and my girls strong. Please let us move forward and still prosper as we've lost a huge part of our lives. I lost a beautiful wife and my girls lost a great mother. Bless my home in the name of Jesus. Amen".

As James finished his prayer, the doctor stepped back over to escort them to Eve's room to see her one last time. Upon entering the room, Lauren felt so weak and almost fainted. She couldn't walk any closer. She wasn't afraid but she just couldn't believe her eyes. Her mother was lying on the bed, stone cold.

Janae reached for her hand and kissed it. She held her hand with her head down and sat in silence so James and Lauren knew she was praying. James stood over Eve looking at her thinking what went wrong. He kissed her on the forehead and began to think about all the memories they had shared. They wanted Eve to wake up so badly and to speak to them one last time. James began to think about the Janae and Marc situation and wished she would've made it to at least clear that up with him. He felt he had no closure.

A few minutes passed and Lauren's phone rang again. It was the same number that called her while she was down in the waiting room.

"Hello" Lauren answered madly.

"Lauren" the voice said softly.

"Who is this?" Lauren asked.

"It's Starr"

Lauren looked over at her father and sister holding each other while they stared at her mother so she slid out the door into the hallway just to check up on Starr. She was shocked she had actually called her.

"Hey Starr what's up?"

"Nothing, I needed to talk to you"

"Well, it's not the right time Starr" Lauren said as she burst into tears, crying over the phone.

Starr was a drug addicted but she wasn't ignorant. She knew when something was wrong with her friend and hearing her cry really struck a nerve.

"Lauren, what's wrong?" Starr asked.

"I'm at the hospital right now. My mother just passed" Lauren tried to contain herself.

"Oh my gosh Lauren, I cannot believe it. I'm so sorry to hear that"

Lauren tried to stop crying but it seemed like the harder she tried the more the tears fell. She couldn't believe it herself. She found it in her to calm down so she could listen to Starr.

"Okay, Starr. What do you need to talk about?"

"Lauren, I want to go to rehab"

Lauren wiped her tears and felt a little proud of her friend.

"Are you serious?" she asked.

"Yes, I'm out here begging people for money and tricking so I can get dope and I got robbed. Like how you going to rob someone like me?" Starr questioned.

"Wow, how did that happen?"

"I had just turned a couple of tricks in a hotel and after I turned the last trick, instead of him paying me, he took the money I had from the ones before him which was only a hundred dollars and the rest of my dope"

"That's crazy man" Lauren said as she turned her attention back to the window to see what her sister and father were doing.

"Yeah, he tried to kill me after he beat me up but he just took everything and took off running

"Okay Starr, I'm so happy that you're ready to clean up. Could you please call me in the morning though because honestly I can barely think straight right now" Lauren asked as she tried to get off the phone.

"Okay, I understand." said Starr as she hung up.

Lauren really didn't want to get off the phone because she was afraid Starr wouldn't call her back, but right now, she needed to be with her family and she didn't have a care in the world for anything else but her mother. Lauren walked back into the room and hugged her father and sister.

The doctor walked in after her and explained to them that it was time for them to say their goodbyes because they were going to perform some procedures that the families weren't allowed to be present for in preparation for her removal. They said their goodbyes to Eve and proceeded out the door. The car ride home was a silent one.

As they pulled into the driveway James grabbed his chest. He told the girls to get out the car and go ahead and go inside but they didn't listen.

"You okay daddy?" Janae asked.

"Yes I'm okay, I'm just having a little chest pain. That's all." James replied cringing from the pain.

"Daddy you're stressing too hard. That's why your chest is beginning to hurt. Calm down because you could have a heart attack." Lauren said as she opened her car door to go help him out the car.

James' chest felt as though it was on fire and he didn't mention to the girls that his head was hurting so bad that it felt like it was going to fall off. He kept that to himself not trying to scare them.

"Come on dad, get some rest, I'll make you some green tea before you go to sleep though" Lauren said.

The girls helped James into the house and felt that he was weak. He put all of his body weight into the girl's arms, barely able to hold him up. They knew he was reacting to the death of their mother. They never saw their father at his lowest. The girls helped him onto the couch because he refused to sleep in the bed. Lauren made him tea like she promised. As she arrived back with the tea, he was passed out on the couch sleeping. She was happy he was getting the much-needed rest and with it being six in the morning, Lauren was about to crash herself.

Chapter 15

The morning of Eve's funeral was very gloomy. James wasn't ready for today and the girls could tell. Lauren and Janae weren't ready either but they knew they had to get through it for their mom. Lauren contemplated on staying in bed but she knew her father wouldn't let her miss her mother's funeral. James was very depressed and it was noticeable. He barely spoke to anyone. He didn't have an appetite and he barely had the strength to get up and go to work. He told his job that his wife had died and they gave him a two-week leave which James was thankful for because he wasn't in the right head space to focus at work.

Lauren spoke to Starr and invited her to her mother's funeral. She was willing to help her out by getting her into a rehab. She wanted to make sure Starr went through with the program because she didn't have anyone in her corner to give her the push or motivation she that needed.

Opening Janae's door, Lauren said "Sis, how are you feeling?

"I'm okay, just ready to get through the day and get back in bed" Janae replied.

"Yeah I feel the same way"

Janae was finishing her makeup not wanting to cry from the thought of burying her mother today.

"Janae I've been speaking to Starr and she wants to go to rehab. I invited her to the house and she can come with us to mom's funeral"

"Well I'm glad she's looking towards rehab now because I heard she's been doing pretty badly on these streets. That's not where she belongs."

"I agree, but I was just running it past you because she'll be here any minute and dad hasn't come out of his room. I don't know if I should give him give a heads up or what."

"It's cool, let her come Lauren" Janae replied.

As Lauren turned to walk out and of Janae's room, the doorbell rang. Lauren walked to the door and opened it for Starr. She was speechless.

"Starr what the…" Lauren said.

"What?" Starr replied pretty embarrassed.

"Girl, you need to shower up and put on some new clothes" Lauren said as she was walked her towards the bathroom.

Starr arrived in a dirty beat up tank top and pants with holes in every place. Lauren couldn't let Starr show up to her mother's funeral that way so she offered her something clean to wear and told her to take a shower. Starr ran towards the shower more excited than ever to finally be able to take a shower. Lauren found a white blouse and a black long skirt for Starr to put on. Anything was better than what she came with. Starr got out the shower feeling like a million bucks and Lauren handed her the clothes to change into.

"Lauren you know I'm really serious about going to rehab" Starr said as she dried off and got dressed.

"You should go, Starr, it's what's best for you right now" Lauren replied.

"I need to get back to the old me. I'm starting to find myself again but I have to pull away from these drugs. The streets are reckless"

Lauren smiled with a few ideas in mind. "Get dressed Starr, were going to get you back to your old self." She began to do Starr's mani and pedi and her makeup. She didn't let her see anything until she was done but when she finished she felt so proud of herself. She felt as though she brought her friend back to life. When Starr looked into the mirror, she began to cry feeling overwhelmed. Lauren thought she had offended her or did a bad job. Starr couldn't believe what she was seeing. She felt on top of the world and hadn't seen herself look like that in months.

"I don't know what to say Lauren, thank you so much!" Starr exclaimed as she gently wiped tears from her eyes and hugged her friend.

Janae entered the room to ask Lauren if she was ready and when she realized the woman standing next to Lauren was Starr, she almost didn't recognize her.

"Whoa, Starr you are beautiful!" Janae said as that was the first thing to come to her mind. She thought about what she had said and if she had offended Starr for saying it in that manner. Starr noticed Janae's face and quickly said "It's okay boo. I know what you meant. I've been beautiful but I let myself go and your sister brought me back to life."

Starr was feeling herself and she made it known. Janae was smiling from ear to ear looking at her friend look the way she did even though she was as skinny as a stick. Lauren was proud of her work but it only covered the truth. The truth that Starr was a drug addict until she successfully goes through rehab.

James finally came out of his room, wanting to see if the girls were ready to attend their mother's funeral. He didn't say much but asked if they were ready. Lauren walked over to her father and gave him a long hug. She could tell he really needed it. James hugged her back and kissed her on the forehead. The girls got into James' truck and started to dread going to see their mother one last time.

James pulled up and got out of the truck to open the doors for his girls. Eve's family, friends and a few co-workers showed up to her funeral to offer their condolences. Everyone was dressed in black and as they were walking up to take their seats, a close friend to the family was singing a beautiful gospel song. It took everything in Lauren not to cry at the moment so she put on her dark shades.

Janae hugged her father, trying not to let go but she felt the weakness in his body that made her almost break down. Family members gave them hugs as the woman sang and individuals walked up one by one to view the body. Janae and James didn't want to view her body but Lauren wanted to kiss her mother one last time. As she got closer and closer to the casket she felt all types of strong feelings. It felt as though God was wrapping his arms around Lauren to make sure she had strength while viewing her mother. She felt as though she could feel her mother's presence at one point but she thought maybe she was too overwhelmed.

Eve was beautiful in her white gown and her make-up was nicely done. She wore all white from her head beads and accessories to her shoes. Lauren just gazed at her mother, apologizing for the things she took her through. She wished she was closer to God like her mother tried to raise her to be and she apologized for that. Lauren couldn't continue to stand there. She was crying uncontrollably behind her huge glasses and she needed to take a seat.

Starr held Lauren and told her everything would be fine and that she had her back. Other than Janae and James, Lauren was grateful for having her friend there to be by her side and support her. As Lauren looked around she noticed her father and sister had broken down and was being prayed over by their pastor and his wife. Lauren wanted to walk over and get prayer too but changed her mind. Starr rose from her chair and told Lauren to hold on a minute.

When Lauren looked to see where Starr was going she noticed that she had gone over to the pastor and asked for prayer.

Lauren was glad about Starr's decision and she wanted prayer as well but she didn't want to ask for it. Little did Lauren know, she had plenty prayer over her whether she asked for it or not.

"They promise freedom but they themselves are slaves of sin and corruption. For you are a slave to whatever controls you" the pastor said as he finished praying for Starr.

As Lauren walked by to greet her aunt she overheard the pastor say "Don't ever stop living for Jesus and promoting purity. There's nothing old fashion or corny about living for God. He rewards those who diligently seek him. The Holy Spirit told me to get that message out".

Lauren felt in her soul that was for her but she didn't say anything. She needed to get right with God but she felt she had plenty of time and a lot more growing to do before she fully committed herself to God. Starr was so done with the streets and she wanted to get clean and turn towards God herself. She would've liked for her friend to join her journey but she knew Lauren wasn't with it so she didn't pressure her but she was going to achieve her goal either way.

After the funeral, everyone joined together for a few moments, outside greeting the family and friends who had come to pay their respects. Many hugs and kisses were given while others continued to shed tears thinking of the ways Eve had impacted their lives. Some of James' co-workers gave their condolences and reminded James of how they enjoyed the days Mrs. Jacobs would send them fresh homemade lunches. They would truly miss her and her kind spirit.

Lauren walked through the crowd, overhearing conversation after conversation about her mother but she was completely in a daze until she crossed paths with her aunt Stacy.

"Hey auntie, how are you?" Lauren asked as she went to give her a hug.

"I'm okay right now honey. I just wish I hadn't lost my sister so soon"

"Trust me, I wish I didn't lose my mother so soon either"

Her aunt looked down and began to rub her stomach "I can't wait until my beautiful niece is born Lauren."

"Yeah me neither. I need my body back as soon as possible" Lauren giggled softly.

Her aunt smiled, knowing how Lauren thought about her precious body, "How far along are you?"

"I'm six months. I have three more months to go and I'm done" Lauren said with relief. "The baby has been making me nauseous again and she's been a very active baby."

Lauren enjoyed the feel of Neveah's kicks and flutters but she was starting to have sleepless nights and she was very uncomfortable at times during the pregnancy.

"Are you planning to have a baby shower?" her aunt asked.

"I did want to but with everything that's going on, I just want to have my baby and that's it. I'm not in the mood for a shower and I definitely would've wanted my mother to be there."

Her aunt gave her tight hug and kiss on the forehead. As they held each other for a few moments, they felt a few rain drops and Aunt Stacy decided to leave the funeral.

"Okay sweetie, I'm getting ready to head home so that I can get some rest. It feels like it's about to rain too and I don't want to get caught in it."

"Okay auntie, I love you. Drive safe and get as much rest as you need."

"Love you too sweetie and don't be afraid to let me know if you need anything."

"I won't." Lauren smiled as they parted ways. When Lauren turned around to check up on her father and sister, she noticed Marc walking up toward them. Lauren immediately felt agitated in her stomach. Janae and James hadn't seen him coming but Lauren knew with Marc showing up out of the blue to her mother's funeral that something was up. He was disrespectful; especially with him standing Janae up when they were supposed to go to dinner.

Lauren walked towards her Janae and her dad so that she could give them the heads up about Marc. As soon as she got close enough to Janae, Janae noticed Marc approaching. Janae was hot as fire but she understood that she had to remain humble and considerate.

"Hello Marc" Janae said as she greeted him.

Lauren kept quiet because she had no words for him.

"Hi how are you Janae" Marc asked nervously.

"I'm doing fine but you wouldn't know that because you don't bother to check up on me like you said you would. You also stood me up for dinner."

"I sincerely apologize Janae but in all honesty, I want to form a relationship with you but I would much rather keep it the way it was when we didn't know each other" Marc said.

Lauren was about to curse him out from A to Z but Janae stopped her, knowing exactly how her sister was. Janae wanted to agree with Marc because things were so much better when they were strangers but she just couldn't wrap her head around why her biological father would have the nerve to say that.

"Marc, if you truly felt that way you shouldn't have said anything in the hospital. You could've told my father and me that you were a friend and kept it that way. Why would you openly tell a woman you're her father and then just leave it at that? That's inconsiderate and it's ridiculous."

"Trust me Janae, it was hard telling you then and it's hard stating how I feel now. It's just a lot going on and I probably shouldn't have opened my mouth about the situation that night."

As Janae was about to reply, James came out of nowhere and punched Marc in the jaw.

"Didn't I tell you to stay away from my family" James scowled.

Marc hit the ground in a daze. He stumbled up holding his jaw checking to see if James had broken it. Lauren pulled her father away hoping to calm him down but she could see the fire in his eyes and just prayed that they could leave. Family and friends stood around trying to piece together what was happening.

When Marc got up and came to, James pushed Lauren to the side and lunged at Marc again. The men in the family took action quickly grabbing James and holding him back.

"Let me at him" James said in a rage.

"Daddy, calm down and get in the truck, let's go. It's not worth it" Lauren screamed at her father. Lauren wanted to do the same thing to Marc too but she didn't want all the drama at her mother's funeral. James stared at Janae and Marc and walked away to his truck. Marc got up off the ground and apologized to Janae one last time before he ran off to his car. Janae stood there in disbelief and disappointment. She knew it was wrong for James to attack Marc but Marc deserved every bit of it. He had no business coming to her mother's funeral with that mess. She felt bad that she entertained that thought so she began to say a prayer to herself and walked to the truck with Starr waiting for Lauren.

As she got into the truck, Lauren noticed her father's knuckles were bleeding.

"Dad, look at your hand" Lauren said as she tried to find something to wipe it with.

James noticed his hand but didn't say anything. Lauren knew her father was upset. He lost his wife and the man she cheated with showed up to her funeral. James was so embarrassed hoping no one knew what was going on. Janae noticed her father holding his head as she sat behind him in the truck on their way home

"Is your head okay daddy?"

"Yeah I'm fine. I've been getting bad headaches on and off for a few days but I'll be okay." he replied.

"It's because you're stressing a lot and you need to calm your nerves daddy" Lauren said as she butted into the conversation.

"You need to go get that checked out" Janae commanded.

The car got quiet and James said nothing in response to Janae. Starr sat quietly in the backseat. She didn't want to intervene in the family's conversation and she had no clue what the fight was about anyway.

"I'm ready" Starr broke the silence. Everyone in the car looked around and said "Ready for what?"

"Mr. Jacobs, could you drop me off at the rehab center please? I will give you the directions." Starr replied.

Lauren smiled and Janae hugged Starr extremely hard in the backseat. James cracked a smile. He was hopeful for Starr because this was his first time hearing a beautiful young lady show interest in wanting to clean herself up after having such a hard life.

"Yes Starr, I'll definitely drop you off there."

As they arrived to the rehab center, everyone got out of the car to hug Starr. They gather together in a circle around her and said a prayer before checking her in. They each gave her kisses and words of encouragement. Starr was scared and nervous because she didn't know what she was getting herself into but she was excited to finally be able to go through this. Life was too short and she knew she needed to get things right for herself.

"Starr, I am so proud of you and I love you so much. You're a true friend and I'm thankful for having you in my life. I'm thankful that you have my back the way that you do." Lauren smiled with tears welling up in her eyes.

"I love you too Lauren. I just need you to turn to God and get back into church. You can continue to ignore him but Lauren our heavenly father has your back more than anyone in this world and with the problems you've been facing, you need him." Starr said as she squeezed Lauren's hands. Lauren didn't reply to her comment. She just took her friend's hand and escorted her into the rehab center to check her in.

Chapter 16

A few days passed after Eve's funeral and the house wasn't the same. Everyone was distant and stayed to themselves. Janae read her bible more and Lauren began to focus more on her future with her new baby. Lauren was making plans to leave her father's home once again so she could get a job and take care of her child the way a grown woman should. James never forced Lauren out of the house and honestly he wanted her to stay but Lauren wanted to be out on her own again.

She was nervous about stepping back out into the world because she didn't have to rely on Money to take care of her. She was now by herself and had a little one that she would have to support on her own. From time to time she found herself depressed and missing Money. She hated that he lost his life before he would ever get to meet his baby girl. She would've loved him having him by her side through this pregnancy and labor. She was down because she no longer had her man or her mother around and all she could do was cry at the thought.

James headaches had become unbearable. He felt the cause for them was more than just stress. He took pain pills and drank tea but nothing would help the pain go away. Janae became concerned and set up a doctor's appointment for so they could see what was wrong and the reason for all of the headaches. She was nervous because of the recent loss of her mother and she dreaded hearing anything wrong about her father.

Other than a few members at the church and her sister, she felt she had no one. Janae prayed over her father as he made coffee for himself before he left for his appointment. James still had faith in God and he knew everything would be okay with the power of prayer. He prayed quietly to himself because he felt overwhelmed with everything that had been going on lately.

"Dad, how are you feeling today?" Janae asked as she finished praying for her father.

"I still have a headache but it's easing up." James replied as he gathered his things to leave for his doctor's appointment.

"Okay, daddy, I'll be waiting to see how your appointment goes today. Drive safe." Janae said as she gave her father a goodbye kiss on the cheek.

"Okay mommy." James joked with Janae for acting like she was now his parent. Janae giggled and locked the door behind him.

James got in his car and left the house to make it to the doctors on time. He knew God was listening to everything he prayed because he was beginning to feel peace within himself. He was starting to deal with his wife's death and infidelity better. He still wished she was alive to answer questions about Marc and that whole debacle but there was nothing he could do about it now except pray and move forward. He would never stop loving Eve, even with her faults. She was a good woman and he knew she had a rough past. He loved her with everything in him but she was in a better place now and he would one day see her again.

It was a rainy and muggy day and James tried to ease his thoughts on the ride to the doctors so he'll be able to focus on what the doctor was saying while there. His mind had been so cluttered and cloudy. The girls would talk to him about things and he could barely remember what the conversations were about. He needed this appointment to make sure he was okay. He had to return to work soon so he could support his family.

James checked into the clinic and felt a strong presence coming over him. He began praying and during his prayer the Holy Spirit told him to stay strong and that he will be okay once he heard the news. James got nervous because he didn't know what to expect now. He remained calm and rested knowing he would be fine. He tried to think of everything possible that could happen in this doctor's office today. He texted Janae and Lauren's phone and told them he loved them and to stay strong, which was something else to Holy Spirit told him to do.

He signed in and waited for the nurse to call his name so that he could go to the back. While he waited, Lauren texted him back and told him she loved him more and that they will get through it all and that he had to stay strong for the sake of his granddaughter. James started smiling as he read Lauren's text and thought of his first grandchild. He had already planned to spoil her like crazy and he couldn't wait.

The nurse called James to the back and once the nurse finished checking his vitals and getting an update as to what brought him in that day, she asked him to undress and wait for the doctor. He was due for his physical anyway, so he decided to knock two birds out with one stone. The nurse left him alone to finish undressing and as James was getting ready to sit on the bed, the doctor entered with his paperwork and a few needles to take his blood. James hated being at the doctor's office and if it wasn't for Janae getting him in here, he wouldn't have been here now. He would've stayed home and prayed it off.

"Hello Mr. Jacobs. My name is Dr. Lee and I'll be assisting you today."

"Well my wife recently passed away and my family and I have been trying to get some things squared away and I've been having major headaches. I've been taking everything I know to take for them and nothing is working. My daughter and I thought they were from stress but we're thinking it may more than that" James said.

"Alright, okay, I'm sorry about your wife and hope everything gets resolved with your family. We'll definitely do a few tests today to see what we can find. First, I just need to draw some blood and then we'll take you for a cat scan." said Dr. Lee.

James nodded his head in agreement and sat quite still as he took the blood. He began thinking about what the Holy Spirit had told him earlier. He wanted to know what more could be wrong and if there was anything, why did it have to happen now.

"Okay Mr. Jacobs, I just need to take your blood to the lab. I'm going to have one of the nurses get you a wheelchair so we can get you down to the scan room."

As James waited for the nurse to come back with the chair, he checked his messages and saw Janae's reply back to him. "Daddy, everything would be fine. I prayed hard and heard God speak to me. Yes, you will encounter another issue on top of what's already going on but he won't put any more on you than you can bear. You will be just fine and you will get through this and prosper."

James felt a strong presence next to him and he couldn't help but to look over. He felt as if his wife was there with him too but he knew it was the Holy Spirit's presence letting him know things were going to be okay. The feeling was a warm and comforting and he cherished that moment.

The nurse returned to the room with the wheelchair to take James for his cat scan. After the scanning was done, the nurse took James back to his room. She mentioned there was going to be about an hour wait for the results of the scan so he could relax and take a nap if he wanted. She handed him a blanket and left him alone in the room.

James prayed silently since he had been left alone, "Father God, this is my third time praying to you today. The Holy Spirit told me that everything was going to be okay. I dispatch my angels in each corner of this room with me and I pray for your protection through this time. Janae texted me what I had prayed about and what I felt the Holy Spirit telling me so I know it's much more than stress headaches that I will hear about today. I just ask in the name of Jesus that I walk out of here today with more strength, wisdom and peace than I've ever had in my life. I pray that you'll help me deal with any problem I may have and that you will help me to endure my wife's death. God, you are amazing and I don't doubt you one bit. I love you father and it's in the name of Jesus that I pray. Amen."

After a while of waiting, James dozed off. The room was cold even with the blanket and after he prayed, he just needed to rest his mind and prepare for his results to come back. James awoke from a knock on the door about an hour later and Doctor Lee entered the room. He showed no emotion on his face so James didn't know what to expect.

"So what's up doc" James asked as he sat up straight on the bed.

"Mr. Jacobs, I have all of your tests back and we have your results. There's no easy way for me to tell you this but…"

James sighed but he was ready to hear the news so that he can get this over with.

"Mr. Jacobs you have cancer."

James had to take a moment to breathe. He needed to let it register because cancer was the last thing on his mind. He had a lump in his throat and he couldn't talk. He waited for a few minutes in silence. Dr. Lee waited patiently as James tried to take in everything he had just told him.

James broke his silence, "I don't understand. How could this happen? What stage is it in?"

"We caught it in the first stages but going forward you would have to take a few sessions of chemo so that we can kill off the cancer cells in hopes to bring it into remission. You're a strong man James and I see that in you. Don't let this get you down. You can beat this and we will walk with you every step of the way. We'll have to run a few more tests on you to prepare you for the chemo treatments so your next appointment will be next week. We'll go ahead and schedule your first chemo treatment in a month so we can get you back to your ultimate health."

James remained quiet but didn't question God about anything. Doctor Lee wanted to console James knowing all he had just gone through with his wife passing. He asked if James had any more questions and left the room to give him a few minutes to think.

James didn't want to let this cancer take over his body or mess up anything in his life. He pondered on if he should tell the girls because he didn't want them to stress any more than what they were already. James returned to his car and sat in deep thought as he prayed to his father once again. He had no choice but to get through this. He had a family to take care of.

Returning home, the girls were waiting and curious about what had happened at the doctor's office. James didn't want to keep any secrets from them because he needed their support right now. It was his business but the girls were grown women now and they could take the news better than they would have if they were younger.

"Hey Dad are you good?" Lauren asked as she met her dad walking into the house.

"Yeah I'm okay. Where's Janae? I need to speak with you two" James said.

"JANAAAAE!" Lauren yelled from the kitchen.

"Do you want something to eat?" Lauren asked James.

"Yes please" he answered as he sat at the kitchen table. Janae entered the kitchen and could tell from the expression on her father's face that he had gotten news that was more than what they wanted to hear.

"Hey daddy. What's going on?" Janae said as she sat at the table.

"We need to talk girls" he sighed as he prepared to give them the news "Well, Girls......I have cancer."

They both sat quietly and stared at James. Janae wanted to cry but she held back the tears so her father could see that she'll be strong enough to help him through this.

Lauren broke the silence "Dad, I'm sorry to hear that and you know you have me and Janae for anything you need. A lot of things have been happening but I promise we will get through this together."

"Yes and with the power of God and prayer, you'll overcome this cancer" Janae said as she smiled.

James couldn't be happier that he had Janae and Lauren for his daughters. He was grateful he had a support system and that they could build each other and keep each other strong.

"I love you girls" James said as he leaned in to hug them both.

"Yes daddy, I'm going to need you to get a little better because my twenty-second birthday is around the corner" Lauren sang as she started dancing around the table. She had gotten James to smile for the first time since they dropped Starr off to the rehab center. She intentionally wanted him to laugh because they missed seeing their father in a good mood. No matter what was going on around them, James was their rock and they would give anything to see him that way again.

"What you got planned Lauren?" he asked.

"Not much but I don't want to be in the house. We should get out and go to dinner or something. Spend some time together. We need it you guys" Lauren said.

"Yeah that sounds good. We do need to do something because mommy wouldn't want us moping around feeling sorry for ourselves" Janae said.

James nodded his head in agreement and smiled at how his daughters had grown into such beautiful women.

"Well alright turn up then!" Lauren laughed as she pinched her father's cheek and hip-bumped Janae's side at the table. They all laughed as the mood began to brighten their day.

Chapter 17

It was a bright sunny morning the day of Lauren's birthday. She woke up to the smell of her favorite biscuits in the oven just like her mother used to make. Janae was throwing down in the kitchen for her birthday breakfast. She had cooked grits, eggs, bacon, pancakes, and biscuits sitting on the table and ready for Lauren to grub on. Lauren wished she had some friends who she could get dressed and tear up the city with on her birthday; she had no one but Janae and she knew she wasn't about that life.

Lauren would call up Starr and Samantha on her birthday every year and they would go shopping for new outfits and heels and enjoy a ladies' brunch. They would end the night off popping bottles in one of Miami's hottest clubs. She found herself thinking about Samantha from time to time and she missed the friendship that she thought they had. Janae tried to wake up early enough to put a smile on Lauren's face. They all had been going through such a rough time that she wanted to brighten her up. She felt bad that Lauren specifically had been going through more than anyone these past few months.

Janae kept her sister in prayer and believed that God would handle everything so she didn't stress out as much as she should have. James was sound asleep that morning after being up all night thinking about the news he had received the day before. He stayed praying and meditating on scriptures that spoke about healing and God as a healer, he wasn't trying to get up too early this morning. The girls didn't bother waking their father up because they knew he needed his rest. He was usually the first one to wake up in the house any other day so they were mindful to let him get as much sleep as he wanted. They wanted to support him the best way they could.

Lauren was super excited and happy about having a family dinner that night even though she wasn't spending her birthday the way she would have a few months ago. This family dinner was something they hadn't done since she was a kid. With everything going on now, she would give anything to go back to those childhood days.

Lauren turned on the shower and prepared her clothes for the day. As she got undressed to go into the bathroom, she admired herself in the mirror. She was showing and glowing with her beautiful baby bump which wasn't real big for her to be six months. Lauren's OBGYN told her that she carried small but it wasn't anything to worry about as long as she ate healthy and attended her monthly check-ups for the baby. Lauren made sure to keep on top of everything except the no stress part. She was so stressed she hoped she didn't harm her baby.

As the days went by Lauren couldn't wait to see her daughter. She wanted to dress her up in the tiny clothes that she and Money had brought before he passed. She daydreamed about her baby's smooth skin and soft fingers and toes and she just wanted to kiss all over her. She also couldn't wait for her baby to come because she felt she would give her daddy life again. She would make him feel loved and help him feel the need to fight and never give up with this battle he was fighting against cancer.

Janae called for Lauren to come to the kitchen so she could eat. She was so proud of the large breakfast she made for her knowing she would love it. She was thankful Lauren made it to see another year due to the life she chose to live. She gave all the glory to God because she knew he always had her sister. She knew Lauren had such a strong call on her life and she's been praying since she was younger that Lauren would eventually turn back to God.

Lauren got out of the shower and got dressed. She went to the kitchen and greeted her sister with one of the biggest smiles she had seen in a long time.

"Hey Sister" Lauren said.

"HAPPY BIRTHDAY!" Janae screamed as she heard Lauren coming up behind her. She put her spatula down and ran to give her a big hug and kiss on the cheek. Janae rubbed Lauren's stomach and told Nevaeh, "It's your mommy's birthday today and your auntie is going to feed you really well today!"

Lauren laughed, "Girl, you are crazy and I'm hungry too. Everything smells so good Janae. Thank you so much!"

"Yes I know. I decided to make you a birthday breakfast to start your day on the right foot. I'll give daddy a plate when he finally wakes up too because I know he'll probably be starving" Janae said.

James entered the kitchen rubbing his eyes, "Yes I am starving sweetie, Thank you for breakfast"

"Happy Birthday baby girl today is your day and we want to make it as special as we can" James said to Lauren.

"Thank you, daddy; I truly appreciate that but we don't have to do much. I just want to spend time with you guys tonight."

James smiled at his daughter noticing that Lauren was starting to see the real meaning of life and not just the materialistic things. He's always wanted Lauren to be a God fearing woman and someday a wonderful wife to a God fearing man. He had faith that someday his daughter will be just that, no matter if she was going down the wrong path just a few short months ago.

"Alright Lauren, we will go to dinner tonight but I know it has to be something else you may want to do in the meantime" Janae asked as she sat down next to Lauren.

"I wish I could go to a theme park but of course I can't right now..."

"You doggone right you can't" James interrupted

"But, we could go to the mall or catch a movie or something" Lauren continued as she smirked at her father's comment.

"Okay let's get dressed and do a little shopping, you know daddy rich" Janae said as she started laughing and headed to her room. Lauren was laughing as well as she noticed her father reaching into his robe pocket.

"Lauren, I have a birthday gift for you" James said.

Lauren looked around because she didn't think he gotten her anything and she didn't expect anything honestly. James took a small box out of his pocket and slid it towards Lauren and she opened it. It was an expensive Pandora charm bracelet that must have cost a fortune from the looks of it. Lauren smiled from ear to ear and she didn't want to be rude but she asked him, "When did you get this for me?"

"Your mother and I got it for you a while back. We were saving it for your twenty second birthday. I wish she was still here to be able to see the smile on your face but I'll be receiving that for the both of us today" James grinned.

The Pandora bracelet had 4 charms on it and he promised her that he would buy her a new charm every birthday hereafter. It had a shoe charm because of her love of shoes, a heart because of the love her parents have for her, an angel because she was their angel and a cross. The cross stood out to Lauren the most because it symbolized what her life should've been like with her family wanting her to get closer to God. Lauren loved it and it made her tear up at the thought of her parents personally shopping and picking out the bracelet together for her.

She hugged her father so tight and couldn't stop thanking him for everything. For the bracelet and taking her in after what happened. She thanked him for supporting her and her pregnancy and just staying by her side for everything. She was thankful for it all and couldn't think of any amount to repay James with the love he had given to her. She didn't care anything about her father's past; she accepted him the way he was and she made it known to him that she did.

Lauren ran to her room to put on her clothes and try on her new bracelet. She was so thrilled to go to the mall because she hadn't been in a while since she was running low on funds. Lauren used to stay in the mall daily buying everything that she felt was worth something. Every name brand you could think of, Lauren had it. When times got rough she even thought about having a clothing sale or something to raise money she had so many clothes.

Lauren, Janae and James arrived at the mall and started looking Janae and Lauren to get an outfit for their dinner tonight. Even though it was only going to be the three of them, they still wanted to dress nicely. The mall had so many people in there that it was hard to maneuver through the stores and really shop. James sat on the benches or looked in the men's stores as the girls went into their favorite stores like Forever 21, Victoria Secret and Guess. They were having a ball together and their father didn't mind spending the money on his girls.

After they finished shopping, they headed back to the house to freshen up and put on their new clothes for Lauren's birthday dinner. Lauren's phone rang and when she checked it, it was the rehab center calling.

"Hello" Lauren answered.

"Happy birthday boo" Starr yelled on the other end.

"Thank you, how are you doing?" Lauren asked.

"I'm doing good, for now. I wanted to escape the other night but one of the nurses prayed with me and for me so I ended up staying" Starr replied.

That was one of Lauren's biggest fears. She had hoped her friend would stay in the program and continue to get the treatment she needed so she could be clean.

"I'm glad you didn't escape Starr. I would've been highly disappointed in you."

"No I'm determined to stick through this. I won't disappoint you but I do thank you for taking me with you to your mother's funeral. It was beautiful because that's what gave me the final push to go to rehab"

"You're welcome Starr. You did it all on your own. You decided to go and you told me so I made sure you stuck with your plan. I'm super proud of you for taking that step. You'll see that it's going to pay off soon."

"Thanks Lauren. Well, I have to go now. I love you"

"Love you too girly. You take care of yourself."   Lauren responded

"I will." Starr replied

"Okay sis. Bye." Lauren smiled with hope as she hung up the phone with Starr.

"Girls, are y'all ready?" James hollered at Lauren and Janae.

"Yes" Lauren replied. She went to the living room with James and waited for Janae to come so they could leave. Janae finally walked into the living room and she looked beautiful.

"How are you going to outdo the birthday girl?" Lauren joked.

"Oh my goodness, I'll go change. I'm not trying to outdo you sister" Janae said as she was about to run back to her room.

"No Janae, you look beautiful"

"Both of you girls are beautiful. Let's go, we have reservations." James said as he grabbed his car keys. Janae loved her sisterhood with Lauren at the moment. They were closer than ever and Janae enjoyed Lauren being back under the same roof.

Arriving at the restaurant, James opened the door for Lauren and Janae as they approached the hostess for a table for three. James gave their names and they were escorted to their table. James had taken them to a five-star restaurant and they couldn't believe the view. There were so many chandeliers and candles everywhere. The lighting was perfect for a romantic date but being that tonight was a special night for Lauren, James made both of his daughters his date. There were many couples out and the smell of the restaurant had a floral scent. The menu had meals they had never heard of before.

The waiter arrived to their table

"Hello, my name is Alex. What can I get for you to drink?"

Janae said, "I would like a sweet tea, please."

Lauren ordered, "A virgin pina colada for me."

"I'll have a sweet tea also and can you bring us your special appetizer for the night?" James said.

Lauren stared at the waiter like she had never seen a white waiter before.

"Lauren, I know you don't go to five-star restaurants much but white waiters do exist. I know you're used to black men that greet you at McDonald's and your little chicken joints" James said jokingly.

Lauren didn't reply, she just sat and watched the waiter serve other tables. He looked very familiar to her. Janae looked up from her menu and glanced at the waiter "Ooh he is handsome".

Lauren overheard Janae and replied "Yeah, I bet he is because he looks just like you". Janae and James looked over at Lauren wondering why she said that and then they turned their attention to the waiter. "What did he say his name was again?" asked Janae.

"Alex" Lauren replied. Lauren thought that he was Janae's brother that Marc spoke about. They had the same hair texture and a few of the same features. Janae didn't want to indulge in the conversation out of respect for her father but she couldn't help but to think the same thing. The waiter returned to the table with their appetizer and drinks and took their food orders but before he could walk away Janae said "Excuse me sir, you look familiar. May I ask you what your last name is?"

Alex wondered where he could know her from but couldn't pinpoint it. He finally answered and said "Christopher. Excuse me I'm needed in the back but I will bring your meals out shortly."

Janae was speechless because she had just met her brother and he didn't even know it. It was so much she wanted to talk to him about and ask him but she remembered what Marc said at the funeral. She wanted to leave it at that. Lauren began rubbing Janae's back because she could tell she was caught off guard. Lauren knew in her heart there was some type of connection when he stated his name but she didn't want to talk about it around their father. She definitely didn't want this moment to pass up without Janae being aware.

Janae kept calm because she didn't want to ruin Lauren's birthday dinner. She never told Alex who she was and he never expressed whether he knew her either. While Lauren was eating and the family was enjoying their conversation, she felt a sharp pain in her stomach and her back. "Ouch! I think I'm having Braxton Hicks" Lauren said.

"Are you okay? Isn't it too early for that?" James replied.

"No, my doctor claims it isn't. She said I'm in my third trimester so I'll have them off and on." She held her stomach as the pains got sharper. "Ughhhhh" Lauren let out a loud grunt causing some people in the restaurant to turn her way.

"Okay, try to get up Lauren. Let's go to the bathroom to get some privacy" Janae said as she stood up and grabbed her sister's hand.

When they got into the bathroom Janae started to time Lauren's contractions. Lauren had Braxton Hicks before but these were strong and she was getting concerned. '

'Lauren, I don't think these are simple hicks. I think these are real" Janae said nervously. "Me too, I think I'm going into labor" Lauren said as she stumbled back from the pain. The pain grew stronger by the second and she couldn't think clear. Janae called her father into the women's bathroom where they now attracted a small crowd to see if Lauren was okay. He picked her up to put her in the truck so they could take her to the hospital. Lauren was in so much pain and she tried her best not to scream. She let out long sighs to help calm her nerves and ease some of the pain. Janae began praying for her as she rode in the backseat with her to the hospital hoping this baby wasn't coming too soon. Lauren thought if the baby arrived tonight, it would be amazing because it was her birthday but it would be scary because she would be premature.

As they reached the hospital, Lauren was in so much pain she couldn't do anything but scream. James ran into the ER and explained what was going on. The nurses immediately rushed her to the back to see what was going on. Janae and James didn't leave Lauren's side and wanted to know exactly why she could be going into labor. James was praying it wasn't any of the food they had ordered.

"What's going on" Janae asked the nurse as she walked into Lauren's room. She told them that Lauren was definitely going into labor. She hooked up monitors to her stomach and stuck IV's in her arms. Lauren still in a lot of pain continued to scream. She wanted pain pills or anything that would help take this pain away.

"Honey, you aren't able to receive anything right. You've only dilated 4 cm and when you reach 5 cm you'll have the option of getting an epidural".

Once the chaos began to settle down, James, Janae and Lauren were in the room by themselves and James started to pray for his daughter. Lauren was scared when she finally realized that it was time and that when she leaves the hospital, she'll be leaving with a baby.

''It's too early for her to come daddy" Lauren said as she began to cry to her father.

"I know but Nevaeh will be just fine. God will handle this sweetheart, just calm down" James replied.

Lauren wanted to know what triggered early labor. She was having such a good time at the restaurant and now she's in labor having her baby. The nurses complimented Lauren and Janae on how flawless they looked. They said their thank you but they were just focused on the baby at that moment. When the nurse came in the room, she told them they were going to have to do an emergency C-section because the cord was wrapped around the baby's neck. Lauren began to cry even more because it was already bad enough that she was coming early but now to hear this just crushed her heart.

Four other nurses entered the room to take Lauren's bed prepare her for the C-Section. "We only allow one other person in the room during surgery" The nurse told Janae and James. They both looked at each other and James told Janae to go ahead and be with her sister because he couldn't have handled all of this. Lauren wasn't mad with James' decision, she just wanted someone by her side that was family; she didn't mind who came in with her.

"Baby, I will be right here when you return. You are in my prayers and you will do great having your child. Your sister will be right by your side so don't be scared or nervous" James said as he kissed Lauren's forehead.

When they took Lauren in the room, the nurses were prepping to begin surgery when the doctor walked in. He introduced himself and told Lauren everything will be just fine. She was so numb; she didn't even know they had started the process. She laid there in tears while Janae rubbed her hair and tried to keep her calm.

After a while, Lauren felt the weight of the baby leave her body while the doctor removed her. The room grew quiet. No one said a word; Lauren only heard water running and the doctor whisper something to another doctor. Janae wanted to know how the baby looked and what was going on. She stood up so she could peep over the blue sheet they had hanging and her eyes widen. Lauren glanced up at Janae and Janae looked as though shocked. She was silent and didn't know what to say so she sat back down without saying a word.

"How does my baby look sis" Lauren asked as she cracked a smile. She was so anxious to hold her baby, she wanted to hop up herself and grab her. Before Janae could reply the doctor came from the other side of Lauren and took her hand. As he was looked down at Lauren, he had he said, "I apologize Lauren, but your baby didn't make it" the doctor said.

Lauren was silent waiting for him to announce that he was joking but he didn't. She was praying he was joking but yet she knew it was a cruel joke to play on someone. A few more minutes passed and no one in the room said anything. She glanced over to see her baby out the corner of her eye and saw them wrapping her up. She didn't hear a whine, a cry, or any sign of life come from. She looked at Janae who had tears in her eyes and she burst out crying, "WHAT? "What do you mean my baby didn't make it? Someone better give me my child" she screamed.

"Ms. Jacobs I'm so sorry" the doctor said as he walked over and picked up the baby. He put the lifeless wrapped up baby in Lauren's arms. The nurses began filling out paperwork while Lauren held her child. She was speechless. Lauren cried hysterically while Janae sat beside her and cried silently for her sister and her niece.

"I can't believe this" Janae said.

Lauren continued crying and caressing her daughter. She had tiny arms, fingers and feet. She weighed 3 pounds and all of her features hadn't come through yet but Lauren could tell she was a mixture of herself and Money. The doctors went to tell James that he could come in the room if he wanted to be by his daughter and grandchild's side. When James entered the room he broke down in tears as he watched Lauren hold his dead grandchild. James walked over to Lauren and held her as she cried with the baby still in her arms. He began to pray. "Lauren I'm so sorry" James said as he continued to cry"

' "See what your God did" Lauren screamed.

James stood up and Janae jumped back in shock to what Lauren said.

"Lauren, calm down. Don't question God" Janae said hoping her sister would take her words back.

"No, forget that. He hasn't done nothing for me but cause headache and stress. He don't love me like he love y'all and I don't care anymore. There's no way he'll let me lose my mother, my child, my man, I have no friends and I'm back living with y'all" Lauren said as she continued to cry.

"Please baby stop. Don't you ever question God and his plans. Don't you ever blame him for the devil's work. In times like this you're supposed to run to him Lauren" James said. He started praying for his daughter because he knew it was a demon in her saying all of this. He needed her to understand that everything happens for a reason and he knew that this moment was devastating but she didn't need to talk about God the way that she did. The doctors took the baby out of Lauren's arms and she felt her soul leaving her body. She couldn't do anything but cry and definitely was done talking to her sister and father about it. They sat with her and tried to comfort her but she didn't want to hear anything they had to say. She lost her baby had formed a bond with that child. It was her baby and she felt no one could take that from her.

Chapter 18

It's been two days since Lauren had been admitted into the hospital and she felt as though she couldn't function anymore. She was depressed after losing her daughter and couldn't figure out what she was going to do going forward. Her body was in pain from the surgery, her mind and thoughts were all over the place and she couldn't think straight. She felt like she lost a piece of herself and her sanity. She felt worthless, helpless and hopeless. As the days went by the raining everyday didn't make her mood any better.

Janae and James tried staying by her side for the time she had to stay in the hospital. The hospital kept her so they could monitor and teach her how to take good care of her C-section incision but Lauren just wanted them to leave. She didn't want to be bother by anyone and didn't want anyone sitting with her so she begged them to please stay home until it was time for her to be released.

Lauren's nurse came in to check on her and tried to make conversation but she wasn't up for the small talk. She just wanted someone to magically walk in with her child and tell her that she made it. No one did that so Lauren kept it brief with any and every one that tried to make a conversation with her.

James and Janae called their pastor and church members to speak with them about what's been happening and to ask personally for prayer for Lauren. James didn't allow Lauren to continue bashing his heavenly father the way she was after her surgery. He was upset and wanted his daughter to turn to God at that moment, not from him. He wished Lauren would realize that he is all she really needs. He's hoping that she'll one day come around and open her eyes one day before it's too late. The world has nothing to offer Lauren but she was adamant on turning her back on God.

The doctor was releasing Lauren today and her nurse was hoping she really paid attention to what to do to properly heal her incision. Just to make sure, she told Janae and her father what to do in case Lauren needed help. Lauren was extremely depressed to the point that nurses came to visit and pray with her. She ignored and acted as though she didn't hear a word they said. They touched her hand and exited the room so they could give her the space she wanted.

Janae arrived at the hospital to pick her sister up and when she saw how blood shot red Lauren's eyes were and how pale she had gotten in a matter of days; she became extremely sad. This was the worst Janae had seen her sister and almost didn't know what to say during this.   "Lauren, I'll help you get your shoes on. It's time to go home" Janae said.

Lauren ignored her and stood up to grab her bag hanging on the back of her bed that the nurse had helped her to pack. She remained silent and Janae understood but she still needed her to say something. She watched Lauren move slowly to gather her things and she tried to help she wouldn't say anything to her. As the nurses came in the help and give their condolences, Lauren ignored them too.

"Lauren, you have to say something please" Janae pleaded with Lauren.

"What am I going to do Janae? Why did all of this have to happen to me?" Lauren asked starting to cry.

Janae didn't know what else to say other than, "We have to pray about it".

Lauren became furious and yelled at Janae, "Get out of my room. All you ever want to do is pray. That's not helping me right now as you can see I'm going home without my baby. I'm going home to no man or mother and to a dad that has cancer. What good is prayer doing for me? Get out of my room NOW! I don't want to hear another word about prayer! Just take me home!" All Lauren wanted at that moment was to get to the house so she could lock herself up in her room with no one talking about pray this or God that. She was done with their God and their prayers.

James called Janae to make sure she made it safely to pick up Lauren.

"Hey dad, I just made it here. We're packing up her things to come on home" Janae said as she answered the phone.

"Okay just making sure everything was alright. Is she okay?" he asked concerned about Lauren's frame of mind after the outburst she had a couple of days ago.

"She's not talking to anyone but her nurses made sure I knew what to do to help treat her C-section incision" Janae replied.

"Okay, well I'm going to let you go so that you can get her home. Drive safe sweetie." James finished the call.

"I will. See you in a few." Janae responded as she hung up the phone.

Lauren wanted to be anywhere else but the hospital or at home. She felt like she could climb up under a rock and hide for the rest of her life. Having a still born baby was really getting the best of Lauren and Janae hoped that she would pray her way through it so she could cope better with everything that was going on in her life right now.

The ride home was silent and outside was really foggy. Everything looked like it was going in slow motion. Janae kept quiet but kept glancing over at Lauren to read her facial expressions. Her face was blank. She had no emotion and it caused concern with Janae. When they reached home, James greeted the girls at the door. He tried to hug Lauren but she walked past him like he wasn't even there. Her mind was so far from reality that she left all of her personal items in the truck. Janae looked at James in hopes that he wouldn't get upset with her. James hung his head down in disappointment and sorrow as he walked to the truck to grab Lauren's belongings. When he came back inside to take everything to her room, her room door was locked.   James   couldn't   say anything. He was a little frustrated that she was pushing them out but he understood that Lauren was going through a really rough time. He didn't want to pressure her or cause her to not feel loved. She needed to see that they love and support her no matter what, so he left the bags by her room door in the hallway.

Lauren lay in her bed for about an hour staring at the ceiling. She glanced over to see all of the things that she had purchased for her baby. She imagined seeing her in all of the clothes, napping in her bassinet, and swinging in her swing set but now all of it was just an imagination. There wasn't going to be a baby to enjoy all of this. She wondered why she was losing everyone around her. She had never done anything to hurt anyone so she definitely didn't deserve this. Everything around her was falling apart and she wanted to run away from it all.

She ignored calls from Starr because she already knew Janae had filled her in on her losing her baby. She didn't want to hear it and honestly, right now she didn't care how Starr was doing in rehab. She could care less about anything that was going on with anybody. A small part of her felt bad for shutting down on her family but she just didn't have anything to say to them. She just wanted to keep to herself.

Lauren was having a real battle of the mind and she wanted all of her pain to end and some time for her heart to heal. Everything was happening so fast and she couldn't handle it. She wanted everything to be finished. She contemplated about her next moves and her entire life. She thought back on all of the trouble she found herself in and almost lost it. She had given herself up for love and was taken for granted, almost killed trying to be a drug boss, lost the man she loved by the hands of his father, lost her mother, and now she'd lost her baby. Lauren began to cry uncontrollably as she felt the weight of the world on her shoulders. This was just too much.

She got up from her bed and walked over to her closet. Searching under a few shoe boxes she had an empty shoe box with her pistol. The thoughts that plagued her mind right now were beyond what she ever imagined herself doing but she felt this needed to be done in order to stop her pain. She grabbed her pistol and walked into the bathroom. As she stood in front of the mirror, she spoke to herself, "This is the only way my pain will ever end. This is all too much to handle. I have nothing else to lose."

She closed her eyes and placed the gun to her head. She wanted to be with the ones she lost. She didn't know how to live this life on earth anymore. "Everything I touch seems to fall apart. I haven't been able to do anything right in my life except lose a loved one." Lauren said within herself as she stood in front of the mirror with the gun to her head. All she saw was pain and despair in that mirror as she cried out harder and louder. She cried so loud Janae overheard her in the next room.

Janae was alarmed at the pain in Lauren's voice. She stopped what she was doing and walked to Lauren's room and knocked on the door. She didn't expect Lauren to open the door for her but she knocked anyway. She didn't want her in the room alone with the way she cried out. Lauren's cries became louder and more painful. Janae knew it had to be a cry for help. She ran to the kitchen to grab something that would pick Lauren's door lock. She ran back to the door and fiddled with the doorknob for a few seconds and was able to get it unlocked. As she entered the room she didn't see Lauren on her bed but heard the cries coming from her bathroom.

The door was unlocked and Janae slightly pushed the door open to see what Lauren was doing. She noticed the gun to her head and Lauren with her finger on the trigger. Janae screamed and bust in the door to tackle and take the gun from Lauren's hand. As Janae tried to grab the gun from Lauren's hand, Lauren was startled, dropped the gun, and fell to the floor crying frantically.

"Please Lauren, Don't do this! What are you doing?" Janae asked as she sat next to her sister and cried with her.

With no response, Lauren rocked back and forth as Janae grabbed and hugged her. Lauren continued rocking in her sister's arms and cried a river of tears. Janae could tell the tears that flowed from Lauren at this moment were tears that had been backed up possibly since the pain of her and Money's first domestic encounter.

"Lauren, that isn't the answer to your problems. This is exactly what the devil wants you to do. He wants you to take your life so you can't live out the purpose that God has for you. You are strong Lauren and what you're trying to do is a permanent solution for a temporary problem. You cannot take your own life sister, please, please Lauren you cannot do this" Janae cried as she pleaded with Lauren.

Lauren couldn't contain herself but she stopped crying long enough to mutter to Janae, "I'm sorry." Janae knew her sister was hurting and she felt bad that she wanted a way out bad enough to take her own life.

"I love you Lauren, we need you sis" Janae said. "Let's pray Lauren, please let's pray. Heavily Father, we come to you today to ask you to please heal my sister from her pain from her heart down to her soul wounds. Please protect her from the devils and demons that seek to cause her pain and take her life. Bring her so much more closely to you father. She needs you. We know you're exactly what she needs. Please bring her to you and please forgive her for her sins. Father, I love you. You can take everything. I don't want it and I don't need it God."

As Janae finished her prayer she felt the strong presence of the Lord within the room and continued to pray quietly as she felt he was healing her sister.

"Lauren I can't lose you" Janae said as she wiped Lauren's tears and rubbed her back.

"I'm sorry Janae; I just don't know what to do with myself. I don't want to be here anymore" Lauren replied.

"If you turned everything to God I know you'll be okay. Sis please pray through this. He'll love you when you feel no one else will. I know it doesn't seem like it now but you'll see as time goes by that he is with you" Janae said.

Janae stood up and took Lauren's hand to take her back into her room. She kept the gun so she could hide it. She didn't want anything like this to happen to her sister again because she knew Lauren would've pulled the trigger had she not made in her room in time.

"Thank you Janae" Lauren said as she got into the bed.

"You're welcome. One question, could you attend church with me and dad on Sunday Lauren, please?" Janae asked.

Lauren didn't reply and Janae didn't want it to force her so she closed her door to let her get some rest. As she pulled the door shut, Janae thanked God again for letting her hear her sister's cries for help because it was no one but God who made Lauren loud enough for Janae to save her. Janae slid down and sat by Lauren's door for another five minutes to say another prayer for her. After her prayer, she went back to her room, left her door open and fell off to sleep.

Chapter 19

Sunday morning rolled around and James and Janae couldn't have been happier. They were ready and hyped to get back into the house of the Lord and were hoping that Lauren would agree to come with them. The morning felt different from any other day. The sun was shining, the birds were chirping, and everyone was in a cheerful mood.

Lauren barely spoke to anyone since the night she tried to commit suicide. Janae still spoke with her and showed that she was going to support her through this. She and James would go into Lauren's room when she slept to say prayers over her. James returned back to work and was happy that his job was able to take his mind off of the things that had been going on.

He was in the shower getting himself ready for church while Janae touched up her makeup and ironed her clothes. She hadn't gone into Lauren's room this morning so she didn't know if she was awake or if she wanted to go to church. She prayed that she would step out and visit service with them because her mind, body and soul really needed it. Lauren still wasn't accepting phone calls. Her phone stayed on airplane mode because she just wanted to be alone.

James was ready for his child to get back to her old self again, at least to have a complete conversation with him and Janae instead of short answers or nothing at all. He hated to see his daughter in this condition. Janae missed her sister more than anything in the world and was very concerned about her as the days slowly moved on by. She refused to leave her room for food or anything to drink. Janae would cook dinner and bring it to Lauren's room. When she returned to get her plate so that she could wash dishes, she found out that the food hadn't been touched.

Janae knocking at Lauren's door, "Lauren, I'm going to need you to come with us this morning. I don't want to force nor pressure you but sis you really need to listen to the word of God. You will feel so much better, trust me please."

Lauren didn't reply so Janae figured she was still asleep. She expected her sister wasn't going to come so she made a note to herself to tell the pastors to pray for her this morning.

"Is Lauren ready?" James asked as he walked out of his room and past Janae in the hallway.

"Nope" Janae replied in disappointment.

James shook his head and had the mind to drag Lauren out of her room but he didn't. He never wanted Lauren to feel as though he was pressuring her to be into the Lord because he knew that wasn't a real relationship. He just continued to pray for her and hoped she would find her way to him after he and Eve taught her the right way to go. James knew Eve would've wanted her daughter in church today and that would've made her proud but instead, Janae and James said a quick prayer for Lauren, in the living, while they were about to leave.

"You got your coat Hun" James asked Janae.

"Yes I'm ready" Janae replied. As James turned the knob to open the door, they heard Lauren walk up behind them from around the corner of the hallway. Lauren had on an all-black long dress. Her hair was in a slick ponytail and she had on flats. Janae and James stopped in their tracks and in amazement as they realized she was all dressed to go to church with them. They were so happy to see Lauren standing there that they didn't know what to say to her.

James smiled at Lauren and said "Baby girl, are your attending service with us today?" Lauren nodded her head. Janae was so proud of her. She wanted to jump all over her and give her all kinds of hugs and kisses but she remembered she was still probably sore from the C-section so she just walked over and gave her a big hug. Lauren hugged her back for the first time since the night in the bathroom and Janae felt warm inside.

"Lauren, you're going to enjoy service. I don't want you to feel like we're forcing you to come but we definitely need Jesus and to hear his word right now" Janae said.

Lauren stayed quiet and everyone walked out to the truck and headed to the church.

As they walked into the house of the Lord, Lauren began to feel a warm feeling come over her like she had before. She felt weak and sick as she walked into the church. Lauren knew it was the devil fighting her to get her up out of there but she refused. She wanted to stay through service to see how it was going to go.

James walked to the back of the church to meet with the pastor and his wife and to get personal prayer. The girls took their seat and Lauren caught eyes with a handsome young fellow. He stood 6'1" and had a light skinned complexion with a clean fade. He had a muscular build and even though he wore a suit, it showed every piece of muscle in his body. He had light hazel eyes and had the features of being mixed. Lauren was extremely attracted and couldn't take her eyes off the young man. Janae realized who Lauren was looking at and smirked at her. She knew this man was definitely Lauren's cup of tea.

Janae tapped Lauren on the elbow and broke her eye contact with the handsome man.

"Hey, what was that for" Lauren whispered.

"You like what you see huh" Janae replied laughing.

"No, I'm good" Lauren lied. She felt bad for lying because they were in church but she didn't want to tell her sister that she was digging on this guy hard.

"It's okay cougar, he's single" Janae said as she started clapping with the church to the praise songs. The music was booming and the crowd was praising. Everyone was so into the word that the pastor gave, no one cared who watched them as they praised, worshipped, and jumped around for their father God. Lauren glanced over to see that fine specimen of a man worshiping as well. He had his eyes closed so he didn't realize she was staring at him again. She looked away and glanced back at him and she caught him smiling at her. Her heart began to flutter. She wanted to walk over to and worship with him if she knew what to do. She didn't join into the worship because she didn't want to fake it. As she watched the others praise and worship, she eventually bowed her head and tried to feel the presence of Jesus too.

The music eventually turned down and the pastor started to pray. The church was silent and when he was done, everyone said Amen.

"Alright, everyone can take their seats please so we can begin." The Pastor said. "I have notes with me today but I will go as the Holy Spirit leads me. There are a few individuals that I need to personally speak on this morning. It's nothing bad but it is something my father wants me to do. Can everyone please turn to James 4:7-10 and when you've reached it, say Amen".

Everyone in the church took a minute or two and then said Amen. Janae looked over at Lauren to be sure she was on track or knew where to look and surprisingly, Lauren was turned to the page and ready to hear the scripture before Janae was. James returned and sat next to the girls and almost jumped for joy when he noticed Lauren with the bible in her hand ready for the word. She looked like she was at peace. She didn't have a mean mug on her face or depressed look. She looked comfortable and was ready to take interest in what the word had to offer her.

The pastor began to clear his throat and he began to read the passage. "So humble yourselves before God. Resist the devil, and he will flee from you. Come close to God, and God will come close to you. Wash your hands, you sinners; purify your hearts, for your loyalty is divided between God and the world. Let there be tears for what you have done. Let there be sorrow and deep grief. Let there be sadness instead of laughter, and gloom instead of joy. Humble yourselves before the Lord, and he will lift you up in honor." After the Pastor read the verse, Lauren wanted to cry. She felt like he was talking directly to her. She knew he was talking directly to her and it was touching her in spiritually in ways she had never been touched.

The Pastor continued to preach about people who needed to turn to God before it was too late because the end was near. He spoke about young killers and drug addicts as well as this generation acting as if they've never heard of a God. Lauren was so into the word she didn't realize her sister and father kept glancing over at her throughout the message to see if she had fallen asleep. Lauren used to fall asleep a lot when she was younger but her mother would always say "At least she's asleep in church letting the word sink in and not in bed at home".

Lauren began to get a little overwhelmed but still tried to keep calm. She knew it was the devil messing with her but now in all of her years of living, she showed interest in what the pastor was saying and didn't want to miss a thing.

Service was almost over so the pastor said one last prayer to let everyone go on their merry ways. The members gave each other hugs. James and Janae couldn't stop thanking Lauren for coming with them this morning. Lauren would've never imagined that her going to church with them would mean so much to them. She gave out hugs to those who came to her and when she got to the handsome man, she froze with nervousness to hug him. She wanted to walk past him but he grabbed her arm and pulled her close to him. He smelled like a million bucks to her and she began to get weak in the knees.

When he wrapped his arms around her body, she almost forgot where she was. Her mind began to daydream and she didn't want to let him go. Being in his arms felt like home. She was so comfortable with this stranger that it felt so good but it felt awkward because he was a stranger. Lauren had no clue about the man's name, how old he was or who he was related to but she was so infatuated with him. She's never felt this way about anyone in her life, and the strangest thing to her was that she never felt like this even for Money. This was something different.

Janae stood in the background as she watched Lauren and the handsome man hug and smile at each other. They had been hugging for a full five minutes. Some of the church members thought they were dating. Noticing the curiosity in the eyes of those standing around, Janae grabbed Lauren's arm and asked for a hug, causing Lauren to detach from the man. He stepped back with a smile that showed all of his pearly white teeth and turned around to speak with another gentleman.

Janae hugged Lauren and said "Dang, if you could make a baby hugging, y'all would've created like three of them jokers". Lauren burst out laughing; a few people turned their attention towards her. Janae hadn't seen her sister laugh this hard or smile since the night she lost her baby and she was so happy to see it.

"He is really handsome Janae, who is he?" Lauren asked blushing.

"His name is Matthew. He lives in the church. That's a real man of God with looks of Gold" Janae replied grinning at her sister.

"Well, he is pretty cute but I'll pass" Lauren said instantly.

"Seriously....you were darn near smothering the boy and now you want to claim you'll pass, Bye Felicia" Janae said as she and Lauren started laughing.

Matthew walked up to both of the girls and said hello to Janae. He never met her personally but he saw her at every service praising the Lord just as hard as him.

"Hello" Janae said to Matthew and he extended his hand to shake hers and Lauren's.

"Hi, how are you ladies" he asked.

"Were good, did you like the service?" Janae asked making conversation.

"Yes, it was very touching. The pastor needed to get through to lost souls but I know turning completely to God wouldn't happen overnight so we'll have to pray for them" Matthew said as he turned his attention to Lauren. Lauren smiled but remained quiet and let her sister do all the talking.

"And your name?" he asked Lauren.

"Lauren, Lauren Jacobs" She replied.

"Oh so your father is James Jacobs, yes he is an outstanding and strong man. I should've known you two were his girls" Matthew said as he smiled at both of them.

Lauren felt he was flirting but then again she wasn't sure because everyone in the church was friendly. Lauren turned her attention to a woman standing next to her father talking and laughing with him. She was curious as to who the woman was because she was draped in Gold and had an all-white two-piece suit on. The woman's hair was long and neat. Her finger nails were clean and polished well. Lauren knew the woman kept up with herself and she really stood out within the entire church. She stared at the woman for a while, completely forgetting the conversation she was having with Matthew and Janae.

When she realized who the woman was, she was surprised. The woman was the same person who walked up to her as she was walking to the corner store the day she was going to cook for Janae. The woman delivered a message from God but Lauren could've sworn she was a crack head. That crack head lady was far from one. She was the pastor's wife and wealthy. Lauren started to feel bad because she didn't want to listen to anything the woman wanted to talk to her about on the streets. She walked away from the woman and here she is, a true woman of God. Lauren was so embarrassed hoping that woman wouldn't recognize her. She looked back towards the two when suddenly her father called her over.

"Lauren, come here sweetie" James called to her. Lauren walked over to the woman and her father and stood there smiling. "Lauren, this is the pastor's wife, Mrs. Harris"

Mrs. Harris extended her hand to Lauren and gave her a full body glance and a smile. "Hello, Nice to meet you Mrs. Harris, my name is Lauren" Lauren wanted to run away.

"Yes, I know who you are. Nice to meet you once again darling" Mrs. Harris said with a grin. James looked confused. "I didn't know you two knew each other"

"Yes, I've met your daughter before. I was around the way doing garden work at a nearby apartment complex for a member of the church who was sick and I delivered a message to her" Mrs. Harris said as she stared into Lauren's eyes.

"Yes I apologize about that day, I was sort of in a rush" Lauren replied. That explained a lot to Lauren about why the pastor's wife was dressed like a bum. She knew it had to be more than a drug addict because the woman was clean behind her messed up clothes.

"Ms. Lauren, would you be joining us next Sunday my love?" Mrs. Harris asked.

"I'll see" Lauren replied.

James looked over at her hoping she didn't embarrass him.

"Yes my love, you should. I could tell you were going down the wrong path and I can tell that you want to explore the worldly things" Mrs. Harris said.

Lauren started wondering why she was talking when she looked like a walking lucky charm. She knew she had over ten thousand on her neck alone of gold. "I see you're looking at my jewelry but see sweetheart; I don't search for the worldly things. I want and search for God so while I'm here on earth he rewards me with the worldly things. I'll give it all up to be with him" Mrs. Harris said as she sipped her water.

"Lauren, I'm going to warm up the car. Have a nice day Mrs. Harris" James said as he walked away.

"Lauren, save yourself honey. Don't end up like my son Christian, turn to God" Mrs. Harris began to look teary eyed. '

'What happened to your son" Lauren asked.

"He lost his life to the streets. He was a drug dealer from around the way"

'"I'm so sorry to hear that" Lauren replied.

"Yes, Chico was my life and I felt like I lost it all after he lost his. God gave me the strength to hold on so I'm fine now"

When Lauren heard the name her heart dropped. She began to sweat and immediately got nervous because she knew who killed her son and why he was killed. "Well you have a nice day Mrs. Harris" Lauren said as she gave her a hug goodbye. Lauren wanted to get out of that church as fast as she could and almost never wanted to go back now that she knew the Pastor and his wife were Chico's parents.

When they reached the house Janae was anxious to get her sister to herself so she could ask her how she liked the service. She wanted to hear Lauren's honest opinion about service and not about her liking it because of Matthew.

"So how are you feeling" Janae asked Lauren as they walked into Lauren's room.

"I feel okay" Lauren replied. She was more concerned about just meeting Chico's parents.

"Well I know you must feel a lot better because you've talked, laughed, and flirted all in the same day" Janae laughed.

Lauren laughed with her but she really just wanted her sister to get out of her room.

"Are you willing to go back next Sunday" Janae asked.

"Maybe, we'll see" Lauren replied.

"Yeah, Me and Matthew both" Janae said as she walked out of the room.

Lauren didn't know what Janae meant but she figured the young man must have said something about her to Janae when her father called her over. Lauren actually felt a lot better about the service, more than her family really knew. She wanted to keep it to herself but she was truly touched and believed God was talking to her personally today. She was kind of freaked out about meeting Chico's mother but she didn't know if that would keep her from the church or not.

For the first time, Lauren thought about dropping to her knees to pray because she felt such guilt on her shoulders. She got up and walked into the kitchen to get some water to take her pain meds and ran into her father while he was making himself a snack.

"Dad, thanks for taking me with you today"

"Oh no problem, I hope you'll come with us again" James replied as he stared at her for a moment. She looked as if she was thinking of something to say. "What's on your mind sweet pea?"

"I have a question before you leave...what did you gain by regularly praying to God" she asked.

"Nothing...but let me tell you what I lost: Anger, ego, greed, depression, insecurity and fear of death. Sometimes, the answer to our prayers is not gaining but in losing; which ultimately is the gain" James said as he smiled softly at Lauren and turned to walk back to his room.

Chapter 20

Lauren couldn't help but to think about what happened last Sunday. Her family was anxious for her to attend church with them again today but they didn't want to put any pressure on her about going back. She felt so good in church last Sunday despite the conversation she had with Chico's mom. This past week had been better than ever and she started to think that just maybe she did need to seek God a little more. Before, she felt like her life had no meaning but after attending the service last week, she noticed that she wasn't depressed. She opened up to everyone more and didn't cry all day and night like she had done the past few weeks.

She just wanted everything to be alright but if it was possible for her to bring her loved ones back she would. Lauren thought about what she was going to do with all the baby's things she had stored away in the corner of her room. She honestly wanted it out of her room because she had no use for them without a baby and it made her depressed just looking at them too long. Her heart was heavy but for some reason, it felt as though her pain was more bearable. It was as if there was a burden that had lifted since the church service. She was feeling like a new person and her sister and father were proud to see her changing for the better.

"Hey sis, you want to ride with me to the shelter before we head to church" Lauren asked Janae.

Janae's mouth dropped because she didn't think Lauren would be willing to go back to church this week. She knew she enjoyed herself because she had seen a new piece of eye candy but she didn't think she enjoyed herself enough to go back again so soon. She was surprised at Lauren but she liked that.

"You're coming to church?" Janae asked.

"Yeah, I planned on going back with you two today to see what else the pastor had to speak about, ya know" Lauren said. She laughed on the inside because she knew she shocked Janae to the core but she didn't say anything because she thought it was funny. "But for right now, I need to head to this shelter so I can drop off these baby items so if you're rolling, let's go". She said as she headed toward the front door.

Janae hopped up and put on her shoes. "Okay hold up I'm coming with you."

When they pulled up to the shelter it looked better than some of the other shelters they were used to seeing in Miami. It was a three story home with a white picket fence. The grass was cut with beautiful flowers planted nearby and had a few well-kept children running around in the front and swinging on a swing set that they had on the side of the house.

Lauren was second guessing if this was the right home because it didn't look like a homeless shelter. No one appeared to be homeless or like they were in need of anything. As Lauren and Janae got out of the car and began to grab the baby items, a woman came out of the front door to help them.

"Hello ladies, I am Sharon and I run this beautiful facility" she said.

"Hi, my name is Lauren. This is a homeless shelter correct?" Lauren asked as she was looked around.

"Yes Ma'am it is. I know you're wondering why these kids and these women are so well dressed and put together. They are dressed nice because I am very particular about what is accepted here. I want the women to feel beautiful and the kids to feel normal. My husband and I built this house from the ground up just for struggling homeless women with children and we were sure to make and keep it beautiful so they'll have somewhere clean and nice to stay. It boosts their self-esteem and gives them hope to come out of their situation. It also makes it easier for them to obtain employment and other services" Sharon explained.

Lauren respected what she was doing for the women and understood completely why everything looked well kept. She loved the house and the reasoning behind it. It looked more like a home than a storage building. "Well, I love the place and I applaud you for everything that you're doing" Lauren complimented the woman.

"Who lives here with a newborn to twelve-month old child" Lauren asked.

"Let me take you on a tour through the house and I'll introduce you to her" Sharon replied.

They made their way through the home and Lauren was in awe. The women were living better than her and they were the ones who were in need of help. She hadn't seen an establishment like the one Sharon and her husband built but it inspired her as Sharon took her on the tour of the home. Sharon showed her the kitchen where once a week, the women would get to learn how to make a gourmet meal by a five-star chef. She took her to the nursing room where the mothers would drop off their babies and toddlers under adult supervision so they could take life enrichment classes, and also the women's personal rooms that included a 40" TV, a queen sized bed and a full closet with a mini fridge to store items they purchased for themselves as many of the ladies received government assistance until they were able to get back on their feet or found a job.

Janae was speechless as she saw how much this woman does for the women in her shelter. She felt that if women could help one another, the world would be so much better. They went to a room where a woman in her mid-twenties was studying. Sharon knocked on the door to get the woman's attention since she didn't notice that she had guests at the door. She was really concentrating on whatever it was she was studying. Lauren realized when the woman turned around that she was pregnant. She kept her room neat and she cleaned up really nice.

She was the same complexion as Lauren and stood at least 5'2. She was beautiful and Lauren wanted to know how she ended up in a homeless house.

"Hey Nia, I have two ladies here to give you some baby items" Sharon said smiling at the girl.

"Hi my name is Lauren and this is my sister Janae. I just had a stillbirth pregnancy and I have a ton of brand new baby girl items. Are you having a girl" Lauren asked.

"Yes" Nia said. She was rather distant and down and Janae wanted to pray for her. Lauren started to think if she should give the girl her child's clothes with the attitude she has.

"What is it all" Nia asked as she got up from the bed and stood next to everyone. She looked as though she was about to drop any day now and when Lauren scanned the room, she didn't see a baby item in sight.

"I have over four thousand dollar's worth of clothes, a bassinet, swing set and baby accessories" Lauren replied.

Nia eyes grew wide. She didn't have anything for the baby but one outfit to bring the child home in and a box of newborn diapers. She started smiling; losing the attitude she had previously when the girls walked in. She began thanking God that they showed up. Everyone stood and looked at her.

"If you don't mind me asking, what's your story? Where's your child's father and why are you here" Janae asked.

Nia stared off to the wall for a moment as if she wasn't sure if should speak about her situation to these complete strangers.

"Ma'am, I don't think Nia feels comfortable expressing her situation right now but..." Sharon spoke before Nia wanted to respond then Nia cut her off "No it's fine, I'll speak. I had a boyfriend who I knew I was I was younger; we grew up together around the way. To make a long story short, I don't have family so he was my family and my financial support. We were together but it was rocky and rough until I found out that I was four months pregnant. He was a street dude and he got killed. Some say it was someone close to him and some say it was a member in his family but I don't know" Nia finished.

Lauren and Janae felt extremely bad for her and wanted to take her number to stay in touch with her. Janae asked if she could pray for her and Nia accepted. Lauren was touched by her story because she basically retold her life story back to her. The only difference is that Lauren realized she had the support of her family. "I definitely want you to have this baby stuff. Care to help me get it out the car" Lauren asked Nia.

"Sure". Nia put on her flip flops and headed outside to Lauren's car.

"Oh your car is nice girl, looks very familiar though" Nia said as she smiled at Lauren.

She didn't think too much about what Nia said because she's pretty sure she's seen more cars like it. Lauren popped open the trunk and handed Nia and Janae the baby stuff so she could take it to her room. Nia's housemates looked out the window in pure jealousy because they never had anyone give their kids thousands of dollars worth of clothes and baby things. The only things they ever received were when the rich white people made their yearly drop off with their old things. Half the stuff that was dropped off barely fit anyone but it was decent enough for the house members to look like something.

Nia was amazed at all the beautiful baby girl clothes in the bags that she grabbed from Lauren. "Lauren I can't thank you enough for what you're doing" Nia said.

"Oh, it's no problem. I hope you enjoy everything" she replied.

Lauren, Janae, Nia, and Sharon had finished taking everything out of Lauren's car so they headed in the house to say their goodbyes.

"Ms. Jacobs, it was a pleasure meeting you and I hope you keep in touch with young Nia" Sharon said as she placed her hand on Nia's shoulder. It was so much about Nia that reminded Lauren of her. Very vulnerable and curious but yet cautious and wore her heart on her sleeve. She was so innocent and sweet and by her thanking God, she knew he existed.

"Alright well, we have to be to church in a little so we need to get going" Janae said as she noticed the time on her phone.

It was a good thing that they were already dressed for church or they would've been late for being at the shelter so long. Lauren hugged Nia tight and told her she would have them say a prayer for her in church and Nia nodded her head and thanked her.

"Hey before I forget to ask, what was your child's father's name" Lauren asked out of curiosity.

"Travis" said Nia as she began to walk back into the house.

"Wow, that's almost too creepy. Your situation sounds so much like mine. My child's father's name was Travis too. What was his last name?" Lauren asked with heart pounding in her chest and praying that this was just a mere coincidence.

"Travis Williams. Why?" Nia asked as she started to wonder what was with all the questions about her child's father, especially since she had already told her he had been killed.

Lauren couldn't believe what had just happened. She believed Nia had to be telling the truth because Money began acting extremely shady when he was alive about 9 months ago. She recounted the story that Nia told them and it was very similar to how Money died. Even though Nia didn't know exact details everything was the same. She knew in her heart that Nia's Travis was her Travis and she couldn't wrap her mind around the thought of him having another child on the way with another woman at the same time she was pregnant. Her mind was racing a thousand miles a minute and she wanted to break down but being in the car with Janae slowed down her tears.

"Okay Nia. Goodbye" Lauren said as she quickly jumped in the car with Janae. Janae didn't say anything on the ride to church because she knew exactly what was wrong with her sister and she couldn't blame her for being hurt. That woman was still with-child and about to have Money's baby. Lauren lost hers and still felt the pain from it. Lauren wanted to crash the car or jump out and kill something. She was so furious; she couldn't think straight and passed the church until Janae got her attention. Lauren barely remembered where she was going as the thoughts went haywire in her head.

"Lauren calm down" Janae said to her as they pulled into the church parking lot and started walking to the front door.

"How you think I'm going to calm down finding out I just gave my child's clothes to a side trick that Money got pregnant?" Lauren didn't want to down talk the woman because she didn't seem to know that Lauren was Travis' girl when he was alive. She probably wouldn't have cared anyways since Money was her financial supporter. He was able to get what he wanted, when he wanted as long as he was supporting her needs. Lauren kept thinking where all of the money was going when they were together and why he didn't want her to touch but only the amounts that he told her to. It was all making sense now. He was paying her bills and expenses too.

"We will go in here and pray but I don't want you going crazy or anything" Janae said as she grabbed Lauren's arms.

As they opened the door to the church, the choir was singing as beautiful as ever. Lauren couldn't pay attention to the lyrics or what the pastor was praying about. Matthew was in church again as well and was staring Lauren down trying to get her attention but Lauren was too heated to even look his direction. She spotted Mrs. Harris as she walked in and waved hello trying to keep her composure but she was pretty sure her face showed every blood boiling emotion she was feeling at the moment.

The choir began a worship song and the crowd calmed down. The pastor then said "I know it's someone in here who's hurt this morning but please know, God is with you. God will never leave your side, just give him the glory".

Everyone started clapping and Lauren began to tear up and felt like she wanted to faint. She stood strong and clapped along with everyone else. The pastor told everyone they could take their seats and as he was beginning to get into the word he paused. The entire church went silent, curious about what was getting ready to happen. Pastor walked over to Lauren's section and put the microphone to his mouth and said "Now y'all know, I let the Holy Spirit lead me in whatever direction he wants. I don't know what he's wanting to do but he's moving in me today". The pastor remained quiet while everyone looked at him.

Lauren sat staring at him like everyone else until he grabbed her hand. He asked her to walk with him to the front of the church. She was nervous and didn't understand what was going on but she followed him to the altar. She thought they had found out about Chico and that he was going to bring that up. She began to think quickly about an escape plan but knew it wasn't going to be a way out without her showing guilt.

"My child, I know you're going through rough times but your father told me to tell you that he will get you through this. He's not going to put any more on you than you could bear and it seems you've endured a lot over the past year" The pastor said.

Lauren began to cry because everything he was saying was getting to her. "You're losing everything aren't you" he asked.

Lauren nodded as her tears started flowing faster and harder. The choir began to sing a soft worship song and Lauren could hear a few people saying "Amen" in their chairs. Janae and James watched with tears in their eyes. Lauren dropped down to her knees and let the floods flow uncontrollably. The pastor got on the floor with her and prayed for her. The more he prayed, the more she cried.

"God I'm done. I'm done. I give you all of me, please forgive me". Lauren sincerely wanted God; she wanted everything that had to do with God plus more. James ran up to the front to be closer by his daughter and Janae soon followed. The Pastor started prophesied to Lauren.

"You blamed God for losing your loved ones, you followed everything but him but I guarantee you he has not left your side. He hears your cries, your screams and even witnessed you battle with suicidal thoughts but he brought you here today" The pastor said.

James started praying harder for his daughter because he didn't know anything about her wanting to commit suicide. The girls had agreed to never let that information out; it would be one of their little secrets as long as Lauren didn't have a desire to do it again.

"You wanted the world while God wanted you. You turned your back on him plenty of times Lauren. You heard the Father but you ignored him" The pastor continued.

Lauren was on the floor shaking and couldn't control her body but she knew she was in the presence of the Lord.

"Lauren, you were going to lose your life if you didn't come to this service today and I'm not trying to scare you, I'm just letting you know what the Holy Spirit is telling me to do".

Lauren felt every word he was saying. She wanted to give herself to the Lord and she was tired of living the way she was. She knew this was her time and she couldn't continue to pass up on it because she needed him. "Jesus, I need you more than anything, I want you more than everything and I will no longer ignore you" Lauren cried.

She had the entire church on their feet crying, praying and praising God. "Lauren, God made you lose everything so you could finally realize he was your everything. He will let you lose it all to get your attention and he has accomplished just that" the pastor said as he picked Lauren up and hugged her.

James and Janae came in and hugged her while the church clapped and cheered for Lauren. Everyone was so moved and touched by the moment.

"Lauren, are you really going to give everything to the Lord" James asked as he hugged and kissed his daughter. Lauren wiped her father's tears and replied "Yes daddy, I promise I want him and only him. He could take everything, I don't want it, I don't need it. I just want Him.

www.ingramcontent.com/pod-product-compliance
Lightning Source LLC
Chambersburg PA
CBHW071954170626
46813CB00005B/1876